ON THIN ICE . . .

The ice beneath her quivered.

A crack rang out, shattering the stillness of the winter night.

Reenie held perfectly still. If I move very slowly and carefully, I can edge my way over to the shore.

She slid her left foot forward, struggling to keep her balance. She exhaled.

So far, so good. Keep moving.

Then she heard another crack. Louder this time. . . .

The ice beneath her gave way with a groan.

She slid into the freezing black water. . . .

She felt herself being pulled down, swallowed up by the lake . . .

I can't breathe, she realized.

She pounded on the ice with her fists, clawed at it.

Where is the hole? she asked herself. Where is the hole I fell through?

She couldn't find it.

I'm trapped. Trapped under the ice.

Her last thought before the blackness engulfed her.

FEAR STREET®
SUPER CHILLER
R·L·STINE

The New Year's Party

A Parachute Press Book

AN ARCHWAY PAPERBACK
Published by POCKET BOOKS
New York   London   Toronto   Sydney   Tokyo   Singapore

This book is a work of fiction. Names, characters, places and incidents are products of the author's imagination or are used fictitiously. Any resemblance to actual events or locales or persons, living or dead, is entirely coincidental.

AN ARCHWAY PAPERBACK *Original*

An Archway Paperback published by
POCKET BOOKS, a division of Simon & Schuster Inc.
1230 Avenue of the Americas, New York, NY 10020

Copyright © 1995 by Parachute Press, Inc.

ISBN: 0-671-89425-0

First Archway Paperback printing December 1995

10 9 8 7 6 5 4 3 2 1

FEAR STREET is a registered trademark of Parachute Press, Inc.

AN ARCHWAY PAPERBACK and colophon are registered trademarks of Simon & Schuster Inc.

Cover art by Bill Schmidt

Printed in the U.S.A.

IL 7+

The New Year's Party

PART ONE

1965

Chapter 1

A NEW YEAR'S SURPRISE

"*F*ive more minutes till 1965!" someone yelled.

The New Year's party swirled around Beth Fleischer, her friends shouting and laughing, the Beatles' "She Loves You" throbbing from the hi-fi— so loud, the whole room shook.

A Coke bottle rolled across the living room carpet and hit Beth's foot. She nudged it aside with her toe and kept dancing. Her new white boots pinched her toes, but Beth didn't care. She knew they looked cool with her new miniskirt.

"Wow!" Todd Stevens shouted in her ear. "Groovy party!"

Beth tilted back her head and stared at Todd. She

thought he looked like a movie star—with eyes even bluer than Paul Newman's. All the girls at Shadyside High thought he was fab.

But Beth wasn't sure how much she really liked him. How could she not like a boy every girl wanted? She couldn't answer that question. The whole thing made her feel weird.

She began to dance again. Then she scanned the room for Jeremy. She knew she shouldn't be thinking of Jeremy while she was dancing with Todd. But she couldn't help it.

There he is, Beth thought. Jeremy stood all alone near the kitchen, sipping a soda. He looks so cool tonight. Why doesn't he ask someone to dance?

Someone bumped into a floor lamp. It crashed to the floor, but Beth couldn't hear the sound over the music. "Karen's parents are going to kill her!" she shouted to Todd, trying to be heard over the noise.

She glanced around the room. No sign of Karen.

Now that Beth thought about it, she hadn't seen Karen for hours. Did she leave? She wouldn't leave her own New Year's party, would she?

Karen and Beth were close friends. They spent hours talking about boys and movies and rock music—especially the Beatles. They made up stories about how they went to London and met the Beatles in person, and all four of the rock stars asked them for dates.

The hard part was deciding which two Beatles to go out with, since all four of them were so far out.

Beth searched the room again. Two boys arm-wrestled over the coffee table, while their friends cheered them on. Some girls checked out Karen's tall stack of records. A couple Beth didn't know were making out in the corner.

But no Karen. Where could she be?

"Fifteen seconds!" a boy on the other side of the room yelled. "Fourteen . . . thirteen . . ."

Everybody stopped dancing. Someone turned the hi-fi down, and everyone in the room joined in the countdown. "Twelve . . . eleven . . . ten . . ."

Karen has got to make it back here in time for midnight! Beth thought. I can't start the year off without my best friend here!

"Five . . . four . . . three . . ."

Come *on*, Karen. *Where are you?*

"Happy New Year!"

Midnight. Cheers. Horns blowing.

Todd pulled Beth to him and kissed her. "Happy New Year, Beth."

But Beth's mind wasn't on Todd's kiss. She was worried about Karen. And she couldn't stop thinking about Jeremy. He must feel so lonely tonight. No one to kiss on New Year's Eve.

"Earth to Beth!" Todd called.

"Huh?" she replied.

"Remember me?" Todd sounded annoyed.

She shifted her attention back to Todd, smiled, tried to act like a girl having a great time on a super date. But her eyes drifted to Jeremy.

A group of tough-looking guys had gathered around him. What do they want? Beth wondered.

Another song started. Chubby Checker singing, "Do the Twist." All around Beth, kids started to twist.

One girl was really good—smooth and sexy. She flipped her long blond hair as she moved. Beth wished she could dance like that. Every time she tried the twist, she felt clumsy and stupid.

Beth checked on Jeremy again. One of the hoody-looking boys grabbed Jeremy's Coke and drank it. The other guys laughed.

"Have you seen Karen?" Beth asked Todd.

"Not for a while," he answered.

"The party is going to get totally out of control if she doesn't do *something.*"

Todd followed her gaze over to Jeremy. "He's fine. Why do you worry about him so much?"

He's not fine, Beth thought. I know him better than anyone—and he's definitely not fine. She didn't bother trying to explain her feelings to Todd.

Todd nudged Beth and pointed to the stairs. "Want to sit over there?"

Four couples sat on the carpeted steps, making out. Jenna Cosgrove had smeared pink lipstick all over Joe Hart's face. Joe didn't seem to notice.

Beth felt tempted, but she didn't want to make out in front of the entire party. "Not there," she insisted. "Everybody could watch us."

"Nobody's paying attention to them," Todd replied.

Before Beth could answer him, a loud burst of laughter distracted her. One of the tough-looking boys had poured a Coke over Jeremy's head.

Stand up to him! Beth thought. But Jeremy did nothing.

She watched him stumble backward, bumping into a girl. "Hey!" the girl snapped. "Watch where you're going."

Jeremy moved sideways, taking wobbly steps, trying to maintain his balance. But his feet got tangled, and he fell, landing next to the food table.

Everyone but Beth found Jeremy's awkward fall hilarious. Even Todd.

Beth saw Jeremy's face turn bright red.

I've got to go to him, Beth decided. She started across the room.

But Todd grabbed her hand and pulled her toward the dark den. "No one will see us in there," he urged.

She hesitated, gazing back at Jeremy. Todd wouldn't want her to try to comfort him. Jeremy probably wouldn't want her to come over. He'd tell her to mind her own business.

Todd tugged on her hand. They squeezed past two boys discussing cars. Beth had seen them around school but didn't know them.

"I want one of those Mustangs," the taller one said. "A red convertible with a big V-8. Oh, man, I'd die for one of those."

"A Corvette would eat you right up," the other boy responded.

"Get serious! All you'd see of my Mustang would be the taillights."

A group of kids began singing "Auld Lang Syne." Nobody knew the words, but they knew they were supposed to sing it on New Year's Eve. The record player nearly drowned them out—Roy Orbison singing "Pretty Woman."

The door burst open.

Beth turned—in time to see two young men wearing ski masks rush into the room.

She saw the ski masks first.

Then she saw their pistols.

Chapter 2

FIREWORKS AT MIDNIGHT

One of the men pointed his pistol at a girl who was by the record player. "Turn that off!" he barked.

Roy Orbison abruptly stopped in midnote.

Silence now.

Beth couldn't move. She kept her eyes on the pistols, afraid to glance away.

"Happy New Year!" the other man bellowed. "Everyone against the wall. Now!"

Todd tugged Beth's hand, pulling her against the wall. She could feel her knees trembling. What are they going to do to us? she wondered.

"We want your wallets and your watches," one of the intruders announced.

Beth unfastened her watch and slid it off. She held it out in front of her and kept her eyes on the ground. She didn't want to draw any attention to herself.

Should I give them my earrings, too? Beth wondered. She hated to give up the little diamond drops. They had been passed down from generation to generation in her family, always going to the first-born girl on her sixteenth birthday.

"Hand 'em over!" one of the men yelled, interrupting her thoughts. "Try anything stupid and this guy gets it."

Beth jerked her head up. Jeremy! He's got Jeremy! No! she thought. Don't hurt him. Please.

Beth shuddered as the gunman pressed the gleaming barrel of his gun against Jeremy's temple.

All the color drained from Jeremy's face. "P-please," he whimpered. "Give them what they want."

Beth tried to catch Jeremy's gaze. She willed him to stay calm. Do what they ordered.

"Don't shoot me," Jeremy begged. "Please don't shoot me." He stumbled forward a step.

Beth cried out.

"Hey! I told you not to move!" The intruder twisted the gun against Jeremy's head.

"I . . . I didn't mean to," Jeremy moaned. "I didn't."

"Yes, you did."

Jeremy shook his head, his eyes wide with fear.

"Everybody pay attention," the robber commanded. "This is an example of what happens when you don't cooperate."

Again, he pressed the gun barrel against Jeremy's head.

Then he pulled the trigger.

Chapter 3

A BUMP IN THE NIGHT

*B*eth screamed.

The room rang out with screams.

Jeremy's eyes bulged. He staggered forward, but didn't go down.

The gun didn't fire! Beth realized. Jeremy is okay! The breath she had been holding escaped in a loud *whoosh*.

Everyone stared at the intruders, stunned, afraid to move.

Beth frantically scanned the room. No one would try to help Jeremy, she realized. No one could do anything.

Then, to her amazement, the intruders pulled off their masks.

Huh? Why are they letting us see their faces? Beth asked herself. Are they planning to kill us all?

Then Beth recognized them. Two seniors from Shadyside High. Party crashers.

The robbery is all a stupid joke, she realized. A dangerous, dumb joke.

The two boys laughed gleefully and punched each other's shoulders. "Do these guns look real to you?" one of them asked. "We bought them at a toy store."

"I knew they were fakes!" a girl declared. "They looked like plastic."

"P-please give them what they w-want," a boy imitated Jeremy's terror-filled voice.

"P-please don't shoot me!" someone else imitated Jeremy, shaking his whole body.

Everyone laughed. Except Beth. She saw Karen at the doorway, congratulating the two boys.

Karen? How could she do that to Jeremy? Beth wondered. She's supposed to be my friend.

Karen was in on the whole thing! Beth realized. That's why I couldn't find her at midnight. She was making plans with these two creeps.

Beth yanked her hand from Todd's. "Karen!" she screamed. "How could you do this to Jeremy?" Beth's face felt on fire as her anger raged.

"Beth, it was just a joke," Karen replied. "Something to liven up the party."

"It's not funny! It was stupid and mean!" Beth shrieked.

I'll never forgive Karen. Never! Beth thought.

One of the boys tossed Jeremy a toy gun.

"Don't shoot yourself!" someone yelled.

More cruel laughter.

With a furious scowl Jeremy heaved the gun against the wall. Then he took off, pushing people out of his way as he hurtled to the front door.

Beth started after him. But Todd moved in front of her, blocking her path. "Hey—where are you going?"

"Todd, you don't understand. I—"

"I'm tired of being ignored," he declared. "All you've been doing this whole night is watching Jeremy. Why don't you let him take care of himself?"

"He needs me," Beth protested.

"Then maybe I'll find someone who pays a little attention to me." Todd turned and stormed away.

I hate him! Beth thought. *I hate them all for what they did to Jeremy.*

Beth saw Jeremy bolt out the front door. She thought about getting her coat. But then she'd never catch up to him. So she ran out into the freezing night.

"Jeremy!" she shouted, her boots sinking into the deep snow that blanketed the front yard. "Wait up! Where are you going?"

He spun around to face her. His handsome face was twisted in anger. "Beat it, Beth. Leave me alone! I'm sick of being made fun of!"

He turned away with a scowl and trudged over the snow to his beat-up Ford Fairlane.

Ignoring the freezing, swirling winds, Beth ran after him. "They were just kidding you. Come back. The roads are all icy. You're too upset to drive!"

"Go back to the party with your stupid friends! Leave me alone! You're not my mother!" Jeremy slid behind the wheel and slammed the door. Snow toppled off the car roof.

Slipping and sliding, Beth rushed around the car and jumped in the passenger side. "I'm going with you."

The tires spun on the icy street as he pulled away from the curb.

"The roads are all covered with ice," Beth cautioned. She fastened her seat belt and checked to make sure Jeremy had his on. "Be careful, Jeremy. This is stupid. Pull over. Let's talk."

Jeremy ignored her. Squinting through the snowy windshield, he sped through a stop sign without slowing down.

"Jeremy! Don't drive like this. Please!"

The car slipped dangerously close to the snowbank at the edge of the road. Beth shut her eyes, sure they would hit it. But Jeremy managed to steer the car back toward the center of the road.

"Slow down," Beth pleaded. She gripped the dashboard with both hands.

Jeremy paid no attention. Trees and telephone poles flashed by in the car's headlights.

Beth studied his face in the dim glow from the instrument panel. His jaw was set, and he stared straight ahead, his eyes filled with anger.

Why do they have to hurt him like this? Beth wondered. Why do I have to be Jeremy's only friend?

The car skidded out of control. Jeremy spun the wheel, struggling to keep from sliding off the street.

"Slow down, Jeremy. Please!"

They sped down the two-lane highway. Beth usually loved to speed through the darkness. It was a great feeling of freedom.

But not tonight. Not on these icy roads. Not with Jeremy driving so recklessly.

Jeremy plowed through a snowdrift, sending waves of white snow flying in all directions.

The highway glistened like silver under the headlights—a solid sheet of ice.

We're not driving. We're flying, Beth thought, feeling the panic tighten her throat. We're flying out of control.

"Jeremy, the road is too slippery!" she wailed. "I'm begging you—slow down!"

"Hey," Jeremy snapped. "It's New Year's. Why can't I have a little fun?"

The windshield fogged over. Beth could barely see out. "Turn on your defroster," she urged.

He shrugged.

"Jeremy! Turn it on! You can't see!"

"It's broken."

"Why didn't you get it fixed?"

"Because I didn't. That's why. Leave me alone, Beth. I didn't ask you to follow me."

Beth wiped the windshield with her sleeve. But it only smeared it.

"Oh, please," Beth begged. "We can barely see the road."

Jeremy tromped down harder on the gas pedal. The old Ford roared over the ice.

I hate it when he's like this, Beth thought. She squinted through the fogged windshield.

And saw the dim figure.

A boy?

A boy in the middle of the road?

She screamed.

Too late.

Jeremy swerved.

Something bounced on the hood with a heavy *thud*.

A face appeared through the foggy windshield. A boy's face, his mouth open in a scream of surprise.

The boy dropped to the ground.

The car rolled over him with a hard bump.

Chapter 4

KILLED

Jeremy jammed on the brakes. The car zigzagged wildly. Then slid to a stop halfway across the road.

Beth stared out the windshield. The headlights showed nothing but the snowbank and the dark trunk of a gnarled tree.

"It was a boy," Jeremy moaned. "I hit him. We've got to go back."

"No!" Beth screamed, her voice full of panic. "Get out of here now. Before we get caught!"

"Beth, we have to help that boy. We can't just leave him there!"

"It wasn't a boy, Jeremy," Beth insisted. She

18

repeated the words again and again in her mind. Wasn't a boy. Wasn't a boy. Wasn't a boy.

"I saw his face."

"No, we hit a raccoon or something." Beth pulled her hair back behind her head.

"We've got to turn around and go back. Maybe he's okay. And if he isn't, we've got to get some help for him. We've got to, Beth."

"You can't!" Beth cried. "You'll lose your license—maybe forever!"

Jeremy frowned. "Forever?"

"And what if—what if—the boy is dead?" Beth stammered. "They could charge you with murder, Jeremy." She shuddered.

"But . . . it was an accident," he protested.

"You were driving recklessly, speeding. It was *your* fault," Beth insisted.

"Wait—what's that?"

Beth heard it, too.

A siren. In the distance. Growing louder.

"The police!" Beth exclaimed. "We've got to get out of here! If it *was* a boy, *they'll* help him. Now, *go!*"

For a moment Jeremy hesitated. Then he floored the gas pedal. The tires squealed over the ice. And they sped away.

This time Beth didn't tell Jeremy to slow down. She watched the snowbank fly past in a white blur, her heart pounding.

She thought she saw the flash of a police car's red light behind them. But when she peered out the back window, the road stood empty.

We're okay, she thought. We're going to make it. We're going to get away.

"I can't see," Jeremy complained. "The windshield is completely fogged now."

"I need something to wipe it," Beth answered.

"There's a rag under the seat." Jeremy leaned over the wheel, struggling to make out the road in front of them.

Beth felt around for the rag. She pulled out a crumpled map, a soft drink bottle, a screwdriver, a Burger Basket wrapper. "Here it is!" she cried.

She frantically wiped the windshield. But every time she cleaned a spot, the fog came right back.

She was still wiping the glass when the car slid out of control.

She saw the look of panic on Jeremy's face as he fought with the wheel, turning it hard, one way, then the other. Trying to pull them out of the skid.

It all seemed to happen in slow motion.

The headlights swept over the icy highway. Then, as the car whirled, spinning faster, faster, the high snowbank spun into view. Then the icy highway again.

Beth opened her mouth in a shrill scream as the car smashed hard into the snowbank.

"Unh." Her scream ended in a grunt as she was thrown forward and her head cracked against the dashboard.

Darkness filled the car as the tall snowpile covered the windshield.

Beth felt warm blood trickle down her forehead.

She squinted hard, struggling to see through the blinding pain.

The pain . . .

She felt another jolt as the car broke through the snowbank.

The car plunged down. Down the gorge beside the road.

She could feel it topple, but she couldn't react.

She felt the warm liquid roll down her face. Felt shock after shock of pain.

The car bounced hard. Rolled over. Toppled and rolled.

Down, down.

"Jeremy!" she choked out. "You've killed us. You've killed us both."

PART TWO

THIS YEAR

Chapter 5

THE BODY IN THE CLOSET

"**B**rrr!" Reenie Baker shivered as she closed the back door behind her. It was only November, but already the weather felt as cold as January.

"Reenie, is that you?" Mrs. Baker called from the living room.

"Yeah, Mom, it's me," Reenie answered. She hung her heavy winter coat on a varnished wooden peg.

"Greta and the others are here. They're in your room."

"Okay, thanks."

Reenie hurried down the hall and into her room. "Sorry I'm late!" she called.

Her best friend, Greta Sorenson, tossed the copy of *Vogue* she'd been reading onto Reenie's nightstand. "Don't worry, we saved you a few problems," she teased.

"Yeah," Greta's boyfriend, Artie Hodges, added. "About ninety-nine of them."

They had a group project due in a week—one hundred killer trig problems. Reenie didn't know how they would ever finish in time.

"No. Only ninety-eight," Ty Lanford told Reenie. He stretched his arms over his head, balancing Reenie's desk chair on its back legs. "I finished one while those two were fighting about Artie's sneakers. He says comfortable. She says gross."

"Fighting, huh?" Reenie glanced over at Greta and Artie. They sat on the edge of her bed—Greta almost in Artie's lap.

"Now we're making up," Artie explained, looping one arm around Greta's waist.

Reenie tried not to laugh. They made such a goofy-looking couple. Artie in his plaid shirt, ripped jeans, hair in a buzz cut, an earring in one ear. Greta in her long straight skirt and belted jacket, every strand of blond hair carefully tousled, makeup perfect.

Reenie could hardly believe it, but Greta and Artie had been going together since the ninth grade. A lot longer than she had been going out with Sean.

"Where's Sean?" Reenie asked. "He's never late."

"Can't start without him," Greta replied. "He's the only one who understands this stuff."

"I think I saw him with Sandi Burke after school," Artie joked.

Greta swatted him playfully on the leg. "Don't believe him, Reenie. He's making it up."

Reenie forced herself to smile. She knew Artie was kidding her. But Sandi Burke could make any girl feel insecure. All the guys at Shadyside High drooled over Sandi.

Reenie knew she was pretty enough—tall and slim with long light brown hair. But she also knew she was no Sandi Burke. Sandi could be on the cover of one of Greta's fashion magazines.

"I'm serious. Sandi was all over him," Artie insisted. "Now's your chance to make a move on Reenie, Ty. Go for it."

"Ooooo!" Greta exclaimed. "You're terrible. Really terrible."

He always carries a joke too far, Reenie thought. She shot a glance at Ty. He smiled at her, but he seemed embarrassed.

I bet Ty doesn't know that half the girls in school are dying to go out with him, Reenie thought. I wish he could hear them talking about how cute he is. Ty had transferred to Shadyside in September, and he still hadn't asked anyone on a date.

"Go on," Artie urged Ty. "Reenie's—"

"Ty, Sean's not working at the Burger Basket today, is he?" Reenie asked.

Ty shook his head. "Sean is off till Saturday. We both are."

27

Then why is Sean so late? Reenie wondered.

Ty let his chair fall back to the floor with a thump. He turned to the trig book, open on Reenie's desk. He frowned. "I finally got to where I understood degrees of angles," he muttered. "Now I'm supposed to forget degrees and start using radians."

"It's a plot," Artie said. "All the teachers have secret meetings. They figure out new ways to make us suffer."

"Trig is an elective," Ty replied. "Nobody made us take it. I guess we can't complain."

"Actually studying this stuff is pretty stupid when you think about it," Artie declared. "How many people out there in the real world worry about radians and sines and cosines and stuff like that?"

"Engineers do," Greta shot back. She sounded irritated.

"Maybe I don't want to be an engineer."

"Right," Greta muttered. She slid away from Artie. "You want to flip burgers for the rest of your life."

She meant that, Reenie thought. She wasn't just teasing.

Artie shoved himself to his feet and strode to the other side of the room. Reenie saw the muscles in his jaw tightening.

Great. Now they're going to start fighting again, she thought. Reenie tried to remember if Artie and Greta had always argued this much. She didn't think so.

Artie flopped down on the floor across the room from Greta. He stared at the carpet in front of him.

Reenie checked her watch. They had to get started—Sean or no Sean—if they wanted to get a chunk of their assignment done. Even trig would be more fun than sitting in a room with Greta and Artie giving each other the silent treatment.

Reenie felt too warm. She wore a heavy sweater over a turtleneck. She pulled the sweater off and started to toss it onto her dresser. Then she heard her mother's voice inside her head. *That's no way to take care of your things, Reenie. Hang your clothes up properly, or they won't last.*

Okay, Mom, Reenie thought as she opened her closet door and reached for a hanger.

She instantly yanked her hand back.

Because a pair of eyes stared out at her from behind the clothes.

Bulging eyes. Blank eyes.

A face, moving forward.

Behind her Greta screamed. Artie cried out in horror.

Reenie jumped back, raising her arms to defend herself.

No need.

She was staring at a corpse.

The body fell face-first to the floor.

A boy, Reenie saw.

She stared at the top of his head. Gooey blood, dark and caked, oozed over his hair.

Familiar hair.

Reenie bent down for a closer look. The head rolled to the side, revealing his face.

Sean's face.

"Oh, no!" Greta wailed. "Noooooo!"

"He's dead!" Ty gasped. "Sean is dead!"

"Good," Reenie said.

Chapter 6

A BREAK-IN

"I'm not falling for that stupid joke," Reenie declared. "No way."

Everyone laughed except Sean, who lay motionless on the floor.

Reenie nudged him with her toe. "You can get up now, Sean. You've had your laugh for the day."

"Come on, admit it," Artie urged. "We had you for a second there. We all saw you jump."

"Well, yeah. You'd jump, too, if someone fell out of your closet!" Reenie explained. "It took me a whole two seconds to figure out it was your usual dumb stuff."

Sean climbed slowly to his feet, grinning. "I thought I did a pretty good fall."

Reenie sighed. "I've seen it too many times. You guys need some new victims for your stupid jokes."

"It worked great when we pulled it on Deena Martinson," Artie told her. "She's probably still screaming."

"Deena hasn't seen it a hundred times before," Reenie replied, shaking her head.

"Maybe it didn't work this time," Greta declared, "but we've fooled you pretty good before."

"Like at the Burger Basket," Ty recalled.

"Yeah," Artie agreed, "we got you good at the Burger Basket."

Reenie had to admit it. They *had* fooled her that time.

She'd stopped by the restaurant to meet Sean when he got off work. As she opened the door, a masked robber grabbed her and told her he was taking her hostage. She could still remember the feel of his rubber glove across her mouth and nose.

Greta laughed. "You screamed that time!"

"Especially when the robber killed me," Ty added. He sounded a little ashamed of himself. As if he enjoyed the prank, but found it kind of childish.

"Hey—don't forget about the time I got you, Greta," Reenie said. "At Artie's house. Remember? I hid in the bathtub for almost an hour. The water was freezing by the time you finally came in and found me floating facedown."

Sean touched the gooey red spot on his head. "Yuck!" he groaned, staring at his fingers.

"What is that stuff?" Reenie asked. For blood, they'd been using a concoction Artie came up with—corn syrup, red food coloring, sometimes a little flour to make it clump together. This stuff looked different.

"Theatrical blood," Sean replied. "I got it at Jack's Jokes. The package claims this stuff washes out with water. I hope it's true. Mind if I use your bathroom?"

"Mess it up, and my mom will kill you," Reenie warned as he headed out the door.

"I can't believe Sean bought theatrical blood," Greta said. She turned to Artie. "I thought *he* had to save all his cash for college next year."

Guess the fight isn't over, Reenie thought. If Artie decides not to go to college when we graduate, I'll bet he and Greta will break up.

Sean returned from the bathroom, his wet hair slicked back. Reenie's mom always joked that a color photo of Sean would be identical to one in black and white. But Reenie didn't agree. Black and white film would capture Sean's black hair and pale skin. But it wouldn't show his blue eyes.

"We'd better get started. We don't want to be here all night," Greta urged.

Sean grabbed his books from underneath the bed.

He thought of everything, Reenie realized. I probably wouldn't have noticed his books with everybody's junk scattered around. But he hid them anyway.

Watching him, Reenie pictured the deep red blood that matted his hair. His bulging eyes. Even though she had known right away that he wasn't hurt, she couldn't push the image out of her mind.

Maybe we should stop playing this game, Reenie thought. Maybe we should stop right now—tonight—before someone goes too far.

"We only finished seven problems last night," Reenie griped. "Can you imagine how long it's going to take us to do all hundred of them?"

Locker doors clicked open and banged shut as kids stuffed their coats in and pulled out the books and notebooks they needed for class. No one hurried. Not with fifteen minutes to go before first period.

"Artie was a big help!" Greta complained, rolling her eyes. "He didn't even pay attention most of the time."

Reenie nodded. She didn't know quite what to say. Artie hadn't contributed much to the group project. And every time he *did* open his mouth, Greta had jumped all over him. Giving him a hard time for slacking off. Warning him that he'd never get a scholarship if his grades dropped any lower. Always in his face.

Greta stopped next to a drinking fountain. She pulled out a mirror and checked her lipstick. Reenie thought it looked perfect. But Greta pressed some more on anyway.

"We had another fight after we left your house," Greta admitted. "I know I've been down on Artie too

34

much. But he's messing up. He spends all his time hanging out with Marc Bentley."

"Didn't Marc drop out of school?" Reenie asked. She had seen Marc at a couple parties and around Shadyside High. He was tough to miss with his muscular body and slicked-back ponytail. But she didn't really know him.

"Yeah. And the creep is trying to convince Artie to quit school, too."

Greta dropped her lipstick and mirror back into her purse. They wandered toward their lockers.

"I don't know what Artie plans to do," Greta continued. "He's changed so much lately. Sometimes I feel really close to him and we have these great conversations. Or we'll go to Red Heat and dance and have a great time like we used to."

Greta hesitated. "But then he'll mention Marc, or I'll mention college—and we're fighting again. He doesn't seem to care about any of the things he used to care about."

Reenie wondered if that included Greta.

They passed the school office. Reenie saw the principal, Mr. Hernandez, talking to a woman in a brown coat. Down the hall, someone slammed a locker door really hard.

"What would Artie do if he dropped out?" Reenie asked.

"Marc is working at the car plant in Waynesbridge. He says he can get Artie a job there, too."

"Wow. What a thrill!" Reenie replied sarcastically.

"That's what I told Artie. But he won't listen to me.

He says Marc makes a lot of money and he didn't have to waste four years in college to get it. Artie's family needs money because of Davy."

Davy was Artie's little brother. He had some kind of a kidney problem. Artie's family must have huge medical bills, Reenie knew.

Greta sighed. "Marc's a really bad influence on Artie. I wish—"

Reenie gasped and grabbed Greta's arm. "Greta— look! That girl! She's breaking into my locker!"

Chapter 7

THE NEW GIRL

Who is she? Reenie wondered. I've never seen her before.

She ran down the hall with Greta close behind her.

The girl spun the combination lock on Reenie's locker, tugged on it, then gave it a hard yank.

"What are you doing?" Reenie demanded breathlessly as she rushed up to the girl. "That's *my* locker!"

"Huh?" The girl glanced up, confused.

"That's *my* locker," Reenie repeated. Greta stood beside her. Both of them stared at the girl. She had auburn hair that fell past her shoulders, and a light smattering of freckles on her cheeks and nose.

"Oh," the girl replied, embarrassed. "No wonder it wouldn't open!" She offered a shy smile. "I'm sorry. Really. I'm new. This is my first day here. I thought this was the locker they assigned me at the office."

"What number did they give you?" Reenie asked.

The newcomer pulled a slip of paper from her purse. "Uh, eighty-nine."

"That's my locker number," Reenie said.

The girl handed Reenie the slip of paper. "The secretary wrote it down."

Reenie and Greta studied the little square of paper.

"That's not eighty-nine!" Greta exclaimed. "It's B-nine."

"You're right," Reenie agreed. "The *B* lockers are around the corner."

The girl blushed. "This is really embarrassing."

"Hey—no problem," Reenie insisted. "You just read it wrong. No big deal. Sorry I yelled at you like that."

"I've made a lot more embarrassing mistakes," Greta told her. "Ask me about the time I went into the boys' locker room!"

They all laughed.

"My name's Reenie, and this is Greta."

"I'm Liz."

They smiled and nodded at one another. Then they stood awkwardly, trying to figure out what to say next.

Reenie saw a boy standing across the hall, watching but not saying anything. She realized he'd been there the whole time.

"That's my brother, P.J.," Liz explained.

P.J. took a step closer to the others. He's as pale as Sean, Reenie thought. And about as tall. But he's so thin—and kind of frail.

"Hey," P.J. grunted, gazing down at his shoes.

Whoa, Reenie thought, this guy seems totally lost.

He had freckles like his sister's, but not the auburn hair. His was ordinary brown. When he finally glanced up at her, Reenie saw that his eyes were a deep mossy green.

His eyes are beautiful, Reenie thought. Too bad he spends most of his time staring at the ground.

"Where's your homeroom?" Greta asked P.J.

He pulled a folded-up class schedule out of his jeans pocket. "English with Mr. Meade."

"Want me to show you where it is?" Greta offered, smiling warmly. "I had Meade last year. He's great if you don't mind a lot of reading."

"Thanks," P.J. mumbled.

"Reading is just about all he ever does," Liz teased.

"Me, too," Greta replied.

"If you count *Glamour* and *Vogue!*" Reenie exclaimed.

They laughed again—everyone but P.J.

Reenie glanced at her watch. "Oh, wow. It's almost time for first period. I'd better get my books. Liz, I'll show you where your locker is, if you want to hang on for a sec."

"Okay," Liz answered. "I could use the help. I'm still a little lost."

Reenie worked the combination too quickly and had to do it again. Five. Nine. Two. The lock opened with a click. She tugged on the door.

Stuck.

She pulled harder.

Still stuck. What's going on? she thought.

"Why won't it open?" Liz asked.

And then it did open.

The door swung open, nearly pushing Reenie to the wall.

Liz cried out and jumped back.

Reenie screamed.

Chapter 8

FAST EXIT

A hand reached out of the locker.

Then another hand. They reached for Reenie's throat.

Reenie shook her head. "I don't believe this. Don't you guys ever give up?"

Ty was crammed inside her locker—his back pressed against one side, his knees jammed against the other. Reenie couldn't believe he had squeezed into such a small space.

"What took you so long?" he asked, breathing hard. He pulled himself from her locker. "I was *dying* in there."

"You know, Ty, I'm getting really sick of these

41

dumb jokes. What if you got stuck?" Reenie demanded. "What if you suffocated before I opened the door?"

"Air can get in through those little slits," Ty explained. "I really scared you that time, didn't I? I had to try since Sean's trick didn't work at your house. You were scared. Come on, admit it."

Reenie couldn't help smiling. Ty sounded so excited. "I was startled, not scared," she told him. "Just like last time. Scared is when you're walking alone at night, and you hear footsteps behind you."

"Scared is when you're in a room all by yourself, and you feel cold fingers on the back of your neck," Greta suggested.

"Yeah," Reenie agreed. "That's scared. When something surprises you, you're just startled. Scared is a lot more serious."

"And it lasts a lot longer," Greta added.

Ty raised his hands in surrender. "Okay, okay. I give. You were only startled."

"How did you get in there?" Greta demanded.

But Ty didn't answer. His eyes fixed on something down the hall.

No, Reenie realized. Not something down the hall. Liz. We forgot all about her.

Liz stood quietly off to the side with her brother. Ty seemed unable to take his eyes off her.

"This is Ty. He's not really crazy. He acted perfectly normal until he started hanging around with us," Reenie explained. "Then he got addicted to our stupid practical jokes. We're always playing dead. Trying to scare each other to death. Sick, right?"

"Definitely sick," Liz replied. She turned to Ty.

"I'm Liz, and that's my brother, P.J. We're new at Shadyside."

P.J. lowered his gaze and didn't say anything.

"I'm new, too," Ty replied. "I started at Shadyside this fall."

"How do you like it?" Liz asked.

"It's okay. I met these guys right off." He gestured to Reenie and Greta. "We hang out a lot. We have a pretty good time."

"It's a little weird the first day at a new school," Liz admitted. "You get all turned around. I even tried to get into Reenie's locker by mistake."

Ty kept staring at Liz. He seemed to have forgotten the rest of them.

I guess all those girls who hoped Ty would finally notice them are going to be disappointed, Reenie thought. One glance at Liz and he's gone.

"If you want, I can show you around," Ty offered.

"Okay," Liz replied. "You can show me where my locker is, so Reenie won't have to bother."

"What was the number again?" Ty asked.

"B-nine."

"It's this way." Liz and Ty hurried off down the hall, their heads close together.

"Come on," Greta said to P.J. "I'll show you where your homeroom is."

P.J. didn't seem to hear her. He stared after his

sister and Ty, his green eyes wide and unblinking. His mouth slack. His breathing suddenly rapid and shallow.

"P.J., you okay?" Reenie asked.

P.J. blinked and snapped his mouth closed. Then he lunged past Reenie and tore down the hall after his sister.

Reenie jumped back to get out of his way, dropping her books. She banged hard against the lockers.

"Reenie, are you all right?" Greta cried.

"I think so," she answered, staring after P.J. He wove down the crowded hall, pushing people out of his way.

"Hey!" someone yelled. "Watch it!"

Greta helped Reenie collect her books.

"What was *that* about?" Greta asked.

Reenie wondered the same thing.

Chapter 9

THE FAST LANE

"**D**o you see who Corky Corcoran is with?" Reenie exclaimed. "Ricky Shore!"

Greta leaned over Reenie's shoulder and peered through the windshield. "Where?"

Reenie pointed to a booth in the Burger Basket. "They're sitting over by the window."

"I think they make a cute couple," Greta commented. She reached over the backseat and grabbed a handful of french fries from Sean.

"How could Ricky Shore be part of a cute anything?" Reenie demanded. "Sometimes I think there is something seriously wrong with you, Greta."

"I *know* there is something seriously wrong with

both of you," Sean joked. "Can't you think of something more fun to do? Even our trig assignment is more exciting than this."

Reenie rolled her eyes at Greta. Sean could never understand why they liked hanging out in Sean's car in the Burger Basket parking lot, listening to the radio, and watching people go in and out.

Reenie stuck a french fry in Sean's mouth.

"You know how much grease is in these things?" Greta asked. She grabbed another french fry from Sean.

Reenie smiled. Greta always refused to buy french fries because they were so fattening. Then she ate half of theirs.

"No," Sean replied. "How much?"

"Too much," Greta answered.

"That's what makes them taste so good," Sean replied. "Without grease, they'd taste like paper."

Reenie spotted a girl with reddish-brown hair hurrying out of the restaurant. "Is that Liz?" Reenie asked.

The girl turned and headed across the parking lot. "No," Reenie said, answering her own question. "Only someone with the same hair color."

"I kind of like Liz," Greta commented.

"Me, too," Reenie agreed. "She's lots of fun. We went to the mall last weekend. They had Scarlett O'Hara-type bridesmaids' dresses in the window of the Bridal Boutique. With hoopskirts and parasols and everything. And Liz insisted we try them on."

"And why wasn't I invited?" Greta demanded.

"You and Artie had plans," Reenie told her.

"Liz made up a story for the salesclerk about how her cousin in Georgia was getting married. She even took down the style numbers and asked about getting shoes dyed to match."

"You know who else likes Liz?" Greta asked. "Ty. Whenever Liz is around, Ty gets a really weird expression on his face. Like he's about to melt or something."

Sean chuckled. "I noticed him standing outside fourth-period math class today, acting real casual. But he kept checking the door. As soon as Liz came out, he walked up to her as if he just happened to be passing by."

"Think Ty is finally going to ask someone out after all these months?" Greta wondered.

"I bet he's working up to it," Reenie replied.

"I think they would make a great couple," Greta declared. "They really are perfect for each other."

Reenie shook her head. Greta loved trying to predict who would become a couple and who would break up. What if Chris and Natalie got together? she'd ask. Or Gary and Randee?

"It's hard to believe Liz and P.J. are related," Reenie commented. "Liz is so cool. And he's kind of weird."

"Definitely," Sean agreed.

"He's not that weird," Greta replied. "I think he's cute."

Reenie made a face. "Yeah, but you think Ricky Shore is cute, too."

"P.J. always acts as if he's sick or something," Sean said. "Like he's about to faint."

"I've tried to talk to him," Reenie told them. "But all he says is yes or no in that low grunt of his. He always seems scared or something."

"He's shy," Greta said. "What's wrong with that? He's new in town, at a new school, and he doesn't know anybody. I've talked to him, and I think he's nice. Smart, too."

"Does Artie know he's got competition?" Sean teased.

Reenie knew Sean was kidding. But Greta answered seriously. "I like P.J., that's all. I mean, I don't . . . well . . ."

"Whoa! Check it out!" Sean teased. "Greta is blushing!"

She couldn't possibly be interested in a strange guy like P.J., Reenie thought. Could she? It *was* true that lately, Artie and Greta had been fighting all the time.

Greta tapped Reenie on the shoulder and pointed to a green car. "Lily Bancroft and Pete Goodwin. I never thought I'd see *them* together."

"Trying to change the subject?" Sean asked.

Greta didn't answer him.

"Where do P.J. and Liz live?" Reenie asked.

They looked at one another. No one knew.

"What do their parents do? How come they moved in the middle of the year?" Sean asked.

No one knew that, either.

A horn blared as a shiny red car pulled up beside them. The driver revved the engine.

"Cool car," Sean observed. "Sounds like a V-6 that somebody has done a lot of work on. I'll bet it can really move."

"It's Marc Bentley," Greta said sourly. "And Artie."

Artie rode shotgun. He rolled down the window. "Yo! How's it going? How do you like Marc's new wheels?"

"Nice," Sean said. "What's it got?"

"V-6 with high-lift cam, oversize valves, and high-compression heads," Artie bragged.

"Wow." Sean sounded impressed.

Marc climbed out of the car. "Come on. I'll give you a ride." He grinned at Reenie.

Marc is really good-looking, Reenie thought. He wore his dark brown hair in a ponytail. And she liked the faint scar that ran partway across his forehead and through his left eyebrow. It made him appear a little dangerous—and older, different from the other high school guys.

"Count me out," Greta insisted.

Reenie shook her head. "I've got to get home. It's late."

Sean glanced at Reenie and Greta, then at Marc and Artie.

"You don't want to go with them, do you?" Reenie whispered.

"I wouldn't mind seeing how that car runs," Sean answered.

"Let's go," Artie called excitedly. "We'll show you what this car can do."

"Hey, no big deal. We'll just go around the block," Marc promised.

"Yeah, just around the block," Artie echoed. "You've got to ride in this car at least once. It's really awesome."

Reenie and Greta exchanged stares. Greta shrugged and nodded. "All right. Just around the block."

"Okay," Sean told them. "Let's go."

Reenie knew that Greta didn't want Artie hanging around Marc. She must think Artie will get in less trouble if she's with him, Reenie thought.

"Climb in," Marc instructed. "It'll be a tight squeeze. But you can make it."

They crammed themselves into the backseat.

"You guys ready for a ride in a *real* car?" Marc asked. He peeled out of the Burger Basket parking lot, the engine roaring.

Artie turned around. "Moves, doesn't it?"

Marc stopped at a red light. A white Mustang pulled up beside them. It had dark windows that made it impossible to see who was inside.

Marc revved the engine, challenging the Mustang. The Mustang's driver responded by revving his own engine. Challenge accepted.

"Let's not," Greta urged. "It's—"

Before she could finish, the light turned green and both cars roared forward, tires squealing. Marc's car immediately pulled ahead of the Mustang, widening the gap as it sped down the block.

"Yes!" Artie yelled, shaking both fists in the air.

He's really getting into this, Reenie thought. She squeezed against Sean's arm.

Marc raced through the next light as it turned from yellow to red.

"Whoa!" Greta shouted. "Slow down, before you get us all killed."

Sean leaned forward. "Cool it, Marc. Okay?"

Marc glanced back at his passengers. "What a bunch of wimps."

Artie didn't say anything.

"Want to have some fun?" Marc asked.

"I want to go back," Greta told him.

But Marc turned onto Park Drive, going south, away from the Burger Basket.

"I want to show you something," he said, eyes straight ahead.

"Slow down," Sean urged. "You're going to get stopped."

Marc sped through the Park Drive traffic circle. They zoomed past St. Paul's Church. Reenie watched the street signs. Bank Street. Hawthorne Drive.

What's going on? she wondered. Why is he heading for Fear Street?

"Marc, give us a break. Take us back," Reenie pleaded.

"This will only take a minute," Marc insisted. "It will be fun. I promise."

Fun for Marc, Reenie thought.

He turned right on Fear Street.

A tingly, uneasy feeling settled into Reenie's stomach. Fear Street had a reputation. A place to be avoided. A place where weird things happened.

Branches intertwined above the street, as if the trees on each side were clinging to each other.

I'm being silly, Reenie told herself. It's just a street. Big deal.

But something inside her disagreed.

"You don't believe all those dumb stories about Fear Street—do you?" Marc asked.

"Some bad things have happened here," Greta said softly. "I saw a story about them on TV."

They fell silent. Good, Reenie thought. She didn't want to hear about all the strange murders and disappearances.

Marc turned left. He seemed to be heading right into the Fear Street Woods.

"You can't drive through here!" Greta yelled. "It's only an old bike path or something."

The car bumped along the uneven ground.

"What are you doing?" Sean demanded.

"You'll see," Marc replied.

"Yeah, you'll see," Artie echoed.

Fear Lake was not a place Reenie wanted to go at night with Marc Bentley. She promised herself she would never ride with him again. Anywhere. Ever.

Marc pulled onto a narrow dirt road that circled the lake. The engine growled powerfully as the car started up a hill. Reenie stared out the window at the woods.

The trees appeared lifeless. Dead stalks sticking up through the snow. Marc pulled to a stop when they reached the crest of the hill.

Reenie knew this spot. They were high above the frozen lake. A short distance to the left stretched a steep drop-off.

"Come on," Marc urged, climbing out of the car. "Let's have some fun."

Artie leaped out and slammed the door. Reenie, Sean, and Greta hesitated, then reluctantly joined Marc and Artie.

"This way." Marc led them through the leafless trees, snow crunching beneath their feet. The moon shone full and bright. Reenie had no trouble seeing where they were going.

Marc stopped. "This is the place."

They stood at the edge of the sheer drop-off. Below them the lake's frozen, snowdrifted surface glowed an eerie silver in the moonlight.

"You've got to get right up to the edge," Marc explained. He stepped to within a few inches of the drop-off and peered down. It made Reenie feel jittery just watching him.

"There it is," Marc announced.

The snow-covered ground was slippery. Reenie had no intention of getting that close to the edge. Sean and Greta stayed back beside her.

"You can't see it unless you get closer," Marc insisted. "Come on, guys—there's nothing to be scared of."

And then his foot slipped.

His arms circled frantically as he fought for balance.

But there was nothing for him to grab except the frosty night air.

His feet slid off the edge.

Artie reached for him.

Too late.

Marc screamed as he plunged from sight.

Chapter 10

THIN ICE

"Marc!" Artie wailed. "Marc! Marc! Marc!" He repeated his name in a shrill, frantic chant.

Reenie froze in horror.

This isn't happening, she thought. Marc didn't just fall over the edge.

But the others were screaming and crying, their faces twisted in surprise—and panic.

It *did* happen, Reenie realized.

But he's okay. Okay. Okay.

He's *got* to be okay.

Trembling in terror, seeing Marc fall again and again, hearing his scream repeat in her ears, Reenie didn't realize that she had moved.

Had stepped forward.

Had stepped to the edge.

To see down? To see that Marc was okay?

She didn't realize she had moved. Until she felt the ground crumble beneath her. Until she saw a rock break off and fall.

Until she felt herself start to slide.

She heard the sharp cries of her friends. But they sounded so far away now.

For she was falling, sliding and tumbling, down the snowy hillside.

She could still hear their cries as she hit the icy surface of Fear Lake. "Ohhh!" She let out a cry as she landed on her back with a *thud*.

It knocked the breath out of her. She struggled to gasp in air. She tossed up her hands as she slid, slid across the ice, slid out onto the frozen lake.

Her heart pounding, her breath coming in short, wheezing pants, Reenie pushed herself up. The ice felt firm beneath her shoes.

She raised her eyes to the hill and saw Sean and the others running down, slipping, tumbling, calling to her.

She cupped her hands around her mouth. "I'm okay," she called back. Was she trembling?

No. The ice beneath her quivered.

A *crack* rang out, shattering the stillness of the winter night.

The ice is thin, she realized.

Reenie held perfectly still. *If I move very slowly and carefully, I can edge my way over to the shore.*

She slid her left foot forward, struggling to keep her balance. She exhaled.

So far, so good. Keep moving.

She dragged her right foot up beside the left.

She stopped. And heard Sean's frantic voice: "Reenie! Stop!"

Startled, she jerked her head up, lost her balance, and fell onto the ice.

Reenie's hip smashed against the hard surface. She let out a small moan of pain.

Then she heard another *crack*. Louder this time.

Closer.

The ice beneath her gave way with a groan.

She slid into the freezing, black water.

Reenie shot up her hands. Reached out. Struggled to grab something. Anything.

She grabbed the edge of the hole. But the ice broke under her fingers.

Hands still grasping, she felt herself being pulled down, swallowed up by the lake.

She went under.

The frozen water shocked her body. She thrashed her arms, trying to pull herself back up to the surface.

Up, up. She struggled to pull herself up.

But her head hit the underside of the ice.

I can't breathe, she realized.

She pounded on the ice with her fists. Clawed at it.

Where is the hole? she asked herself. Where is the hole I fell through?

Where?

She couldn't find it.

I'm trapped. Trapped under the ice.

Her last thought before the blackness engulfed her.

Chapter 11

"I THINK HE KNOWS"

I can't breathe.

Reenie gasped for air.

She choked. Coughed up water.

Reenie could hear Sean's voice. He sounded so far away.

"You're all right, Reenie," Sean was saying. "You're all right."

She opened her eyes and found Sean leaning over her. His face inches from hers.

"I thought . . . I thought that you had drowned." Sean's voice shook. He straightened up, and Reenie saw Artie and Greta behind him.

"Sean saved you," Greta explained. "He reached in

and pulled you out. Then he gave you mouth-to-mouth."

"That was the fun part," Sean joked. But Reenie noticed his voice still didn't sound quite steady.

Reenie forced herself to sit up. "What happened to Marc? Is he okay?"

"I'm right here." A low voice from behind her.

Reenie turned—and pain jarred her temples.

Marc met her gaze. "Sorry," he muttered. "It was just a dumb joke."

"And Artie helped him plan it!" Greta chimed in angrily. "He told Marc about the jokes we play on each other, and they planned the whole thing."

"Hey, come on, guys. We didn't mean for anyone to get hurt," Artie insisted. "Marc and I go down that hill all the time—just for fun. It's like a big snow slide. When Marc faked that fall, he just slid to the bottom."

Artie turned to Greta. "We never slid that far out on the ice. Really. I don't know what happened. . . ." His voice trailed off.

"Can you stand up?" Sean asked Reenie.

Reenie groaned. "I'll try."

Sean grabbed her hands and slowly pulled her to her feet. Reenie's legs trembled, but she kept her balance.

"Give me your coats," Sean ordered the others. "Reenie is freezing."

Sean yanked off his own coat and wrapped it around her. Then he layered the other coats on top.

A shudder shook Reenie's whole body. She couldn't feel her hands and feet. Totally numb.

Sean wrapped his arm around her waist. "Let's get you home so you can get into some dry clothes and warm up."

Greta hurried to Reenie's other side and grabbed her arm. "Wow. I'm glad you're okay. I was really scared," Greta told her.

"Follow me," Artie said. "There's a place over here where we can climb back up."

Reenie's teeth were chattering by the time she reached the car. Marc cranked the heater up full blast, but she couldn't stop shivering.

I had the strongest feeling that something bad would happen if we kept playing the dumb jokes on each other, Reenie remembered. Sure enough, something bad happened to me.

Now, is this the end of it?

"Sean called to you because he knew if you kept trying to walk, the ice would crack," Greta told Reenie in the cafeteria the next day. "When you fell, he got flat on the ice. Then he sort of wiggled and slid himself up to the hole so he could reach in and grab you."

Greta shivered. "I was so scared. And we couldn't help him. We were afraid the ice would break if we got too close."

Reenie took a bite of salad. "I can hardly believe it really happened," she told Greta.

"Well, it did. And it was Artie's fault."

Reenie saw Sean with his lunch tray. She waved and pointed to the empty seat across from her.

"Artie had no way of knowing I'd slip and fall," she reminded her friend.

Sean slid into the spot next to Greta.

"It was still a horrible thing to do," Greta insisted.

"What?" Sean asked. He scooped up a forkful of bright orange macaroni and cheese.

"Greta's furious at Artie for what happened yesterday," Reenie replied.

"It was an accident," Sean protested.

Greta leaped to her feet. "I'm going to go get an ice-cream bar," Greta announced. "I'll be right back."

She must be really upset, Reenie thought. Greta hardly ever ate dessert. But when she felt bad, she always headed for chocolate.

"What's her problem?" Sean asked.

"She and Artie are always fighting," Reenie told him. "She hates the way he acts when he hangs out with Marc Bentley. She's afraid Artie might drop out of school and get a job where Marc works."

"Could happen, I guess. Artie's family needs cash right now. But Artie hasn't mentioned dropping out to me." Sean shoveled in more of the macaroni and cheese.

Reenie played with her salad, pushing the celery and carrots into separate piles with her fork. She wasn't hungry. She kept remembering the panic she felt when she struggled to the surface of Fear Lake— and hit the wall of ice.

She couldn't force it from her mind.

Reenie glanced up at Sean and found him staring over her shoulder with an odd expression on his face. "Check it out," he murmured.

Reenie turned and scanned the room. At first she couldn't figure out what Sean wanted her to see. Then she saw Greta and P.J. standing close together at the back of the lunchroom. So engrossed in conversation they seemed unaware of anything but each other.

Sean turned back to Reenie. "I don't believe it," he whispered. "Greta and P.J. Is that a weird couple—or what?"

"She likes weird guys. What can I say?" Reenie risked another quick peek at Greta and P.J. Greta was laughing hard, and P.J. appeared pleased with himself.

"I think Artie and Greta will make up," Reenie declared. "They've been going together forever."

"Maybe," Sean agreed. "But Artie is not going to be too happy if he finds Greta flirting with another guy."

"Uh-oh," Reenie whispered. "I think he knows."

She nodded toward the big double doors at the front of the cafeteria.

Artie stood there, glaring across the room at Greta and P.J. His hands clenched into fists. His face taut with anger.

Reenie raised a hand to her mouth as she watched Artie lurch toward Greta and P.J.

Please don't do anything stupid, Reenie silently begged.

Chapter 12

DANGER AHEAD

"**I**'ve got to stop him," Sean told her. He jumped to his feet and hurried over to Artie.

Reenie kept her eyes on Greta. Greta hadn't noticed Artie yet. She tenderly brushed a lock of hair off P.J.'s forehead and smiled at him.

Reenie turned back toward Artie. Sean appeared to be calming Artie down. Artie's hands relaxed at his sides. His face returned to its usual color. Then Sean slapped him on the shoulder, and Artie whirled around and stalked out the double doors of the cafeteria.

Sean knew exactly what to say to him, Reenie thought. But I'll bet Greta and Artie will have a huge fight the next time they are together. I hope I'm not around to watch it.

"I thought Artie was going to go ballistic!" Sean exclaimed as he sat back down across from Reenie. "I told him he'd look like a jerk if he got into a fight in the lunchroom.

"Wow. He looked scary," Reenie said. "I wouldn't want Artie mad at *me!*"

The bell rang, and Sean chugged the rest of his soda. "Remember, I can't drive you home today," he told her. "I have a chess club meeting."

Not exactly walking weather, Reenie thought after her last class. Dark and wet out. It will probably snow before I make it home.

She wandered over to the student parking lot, hoping she could find someone to give her a ride.

Reenie gasped as she felt a cold, damp hand squeeze her neck. She spun around and found Liz grinning at her.

"Sorry, I couldn't resist," Liz told her.

"Aren't you freezing?" Reenie demanded. Every button on Liz's coat was open. And she wasn't wearing a sweater—only a thin blouse.

"No," Liz answered. "I love the cold."

Reenie hated gray winter days. They seemed to wash the color out of everything.

Everything except Liz's hair, Reenie noticed. I'd kill for hair like that, she thought. All those coppery highlights.

"I heard what happened to you yesterday!" Liz exclaimed. "Wow. Scary."

"Really scary," Reenie declared. "How are you and P.J. doing at Shadyside?" she asked, changing the subject. She didn't want to think about the accident.

"Great," Liz answered. "It's hard to believe I didn't know anyone but P.J. a month ago."

Reenie found it hard to believe, too. Liz had become a good friend. Reenie felt as though she had known Liz for much longer than a month.

"Well, I guess P.J.'s not exactly doing so great," Liz confessed. "He's so awkward and shy. It's hard for him to approach people."

"I've noticed," Reenie commented.

"It's not really P.J.'s fault, you know," Liz said.

Not sure what to say, Reenie didn't respond. They started across the parking lot, slipping between a Jeep and an old Chevy.

"P.J.'s not well," Liz went on.

"What's wrong with him?"

"He's frail. He can't do physical things."

"Maybe he should work out or something—build up his strength," Reenie suggested.

"You don't understand. He's got a heart murmur. He can't work out or anything like that. He's excused from PE."

"How . . . how serious is it?"

"He's okay as long as he doesn't do physical stuff."

Reenie felt guilty for all the mean things she had been thinking about P.J. She decided to try to make him feel more welcome at Shadyside High.

"Greta and P.J. seem to have a lot to talk about," Reenie observed.

"I wish he would ask her out. But I'm afraid he's too shy. He's never worked up the courage to ask any girl out."

"He's never gone out with a girl—ever?" Reenie asked, surprised.

"Never. But don't tell anyone, okay? P.J. would be really bummed if it got around."

"I won't," Reenie promised. "I think it would be great for P.J. to go out with someone," Reenie continued slowly. "But Greta's still going with Artie, so . . ."

Reenie heard footsteps behind her and turned around. She found Ty hurrying to catch up to them.

"Hey. Where you guys headed?" he called breathlessly.

"Nowhere special," Liz replied.

Ty has a car, Reenie remembered. At last. A ride.

"Liz . . ." Ty hesitated.

"Uh-huh?"

"Could I ask you something?"

Oh, no, Reenie thought. Ty's finally decided to ask Liz out, and I'm standing here like her chaperon.

She checked her watch. "Listen, you guys, I've got to run. I'll catch you later, okay?"

"Okay," Liz replied. "See you tomorrow."

"Later," Ty said.

Reenie moved deeper into the parking lot. It's emptying out fast, she thought. Isn't there anyone here I can catch a ride with?

A red car squealed to a stop in front of her. Marc Bentley's red car.

I'd rather freeze to death, Reenie told herself.

Artie rolled down the window. "Reenie—yo! Look what I'm driving. Need a ride?"

"No, thanks," Reenie called. Even without Marc behind the wheel, she didn't want another ride in the red car. "I think I'm going to walk. I need the exercise."

"It's going to storm," Artie warned.

A gust of wind sent freezing air down the back of her coat collar. She shivered, the chill reminding her of last night. The frigid water of Fear Lake.

Knowing she was going to drown.

"Hop in," Artie urged.

Reenie glanced around the parking lot. Artie's my only chance for a ride. "Okay," Reenie answered reluctantly. She climbed in.

"Where's Greta this afternoon?" Reenie asked. Artie scowled. Dumb question, she thought. Dumb, dumb, dumb.

"She brought her own car today," Artie replied through clenched teeth. He peeled out of the exit and roared away from the school.

I wish I'd known that, Reenie thought. I could have ridden home with her. Reenie realized she'd barely spoken to Greta the entire day—just those few minutes in the cafeteria.

Artie pushed down on the gas. Reenie made sure her seat belt was fastened properly. Artie's driving made her nervous.

Artie pulled to a stop in front of a red light. "Hey, Reenie . . ."

"What?"

"Last night . . . you know. I didn't mean for you to fall."

Reenie sighed. "I know."

"I wanted to go out on the ice with Sean. Help pull you up. But we thought the ice might break some more."

"I know that, Artie."

"Good. Watch this." The light turned green. Artie floored the gas pedal. The tires squealed as the powerful car shot forward.

"Artie, don't!"

"It's okay, Reenie!" Artie yelled. "I drive a lot better than Marc!"

Artie sped down the road into another intersection. Horns blared. Tires squealed.

"Look out!" Reenie shrieked.

Chapter 13

NOT P.J.!

Reenie's scream stuck in her throat.

She heard metal slam against metal. Shattering glass.

The car spun, slamming her into the door.

She heard someone screaming. Far away.

Felt the seat belt biting into her stomach, as she was thrown forward. Then she lurched back against the seat.

Reenie tasted blood in her mouth. Metallic and salty.

I bit my tongue, she realized. That's all. I just bit my tongue.

The car shuddered to a stop.

"You okay?" Artie groaned.

"Yeah—I think so." Reenie peered out the window. She couldn't see much. Cracks covered the glass like a huge spiderweb.

She shoved open the door and leaned out. A sharp, sour taste hit the back of her throat. She swallowed hard.

A green van had smashed into the rear door. On *my side,* Reenie thought. Two feet from where I'm sitting.

Reenie slowly climbed out of the car. Her legs felt as though she had run up and down the gym bleachers a hundred times. They wouldn't stop trembling.

Artie hurried over to Reenie. "Oh, wow!" Artie groaned, staring at the caved-in door. "Marc is going to kill me."

Where's the van driver? Reenie wondered.

Then she saw him. Still in the van. A dark shape slumped over the wheel.

"Hey, are you okay?" she called.

The driver didn't reply. Didn't move.

"Are you okay?" Reenie called again. Oh, no. I hope he's not hurt, Reenie thought. She hurried to the van and yanked open the door. Gently she pulled the driver back against the seat.

She sucked in her breath.

"Huh?" A startled cry escaped her lips as she saw his face.

P.J.! The van driver was P.J.

Reenie remembered what Liz told her—about P.J.'s having a heart murmur. She felt for his pulse. "Please be all right. Please!" she begged.

P.J.'s eyes fluttered open and he turned his head toward Reenie. "Are you hurt?" she cried.

But he didn't answer. He seemed totally bewildered. Barely conscious.

"Oh, no, I don't *believe* it!" Artie cried, striding up beside Reenie.

"Artie—he's hurt," Reenie said.

"You creep!" he snarled at P.J. "Look what you did! You plowed right into me. Marc's going to kill me!"

P.J. didn't react.

He's still dazed, Reenie saw.

Artie slammed the side of the van with his fist. "You ran a stop sign!" he screamed. "Don't you know how to drive? What's wrong with you!"

Reenie slipped between Artie and P.J. "Calm down," she urged. "Please."

Artie grabbed her by the shoulders. He stared at her, his eyes cold. "Why is everyone always defending him?" he demanded. "What's so special about P.J.?" Artie's fingers dug into her skin. She could feel his hot breath on her face. "Huh, Reenie? Why does everyone love little P.J.?"

Reenie didn't answer. She concentrated on meeting Artie's gaze. She knew if Artie decided to go for P.J., she wouldn't be able to stop him.

Artie, leave P.J. alone, she thought. Leave him alone. It's not his fault you and Greta are always fighting.

A horn honked behind them—loud and long.

Artie let go of Reenie and backed away, shaking his head.

72

Whew! That was close, Reenie thought. Relief raced through her as she watched Artie climb back into the car.

Artie stuck his head out the window. "I'm not going to forget this, P.J.!" he yelled. Then he peeled away, his tires squealing.

Reenie turned to P.J. "Are you okay?" she asked softly. He nodded. His eyes seemed clearer. "Okay as I'll ever be," he told her glumly.

"Marc went totally ballistic over what Artie did to his car," Greta told the others the next day at lunch.

"I don't blame him," Sean muttered.

"It wasn't Artie's fault," Reenie reminded them. "P.J. ran the stop sign."

Reenie noticed Liz staring down at her plate. Poor Liz, she thought. It must be tough having a brother like P.J. She must feel she has to protect him all the time.

Reenie glanced over at Liz. Ty was leaning close to her, whispering something that made Liz smile a little. Reenie smiled, too. At least Liz and Ty are getting together, she thought. Now maybe Liz won't worry about P.J. *all* the time.

"Ever since Artie started running around with Marc, he acts crazy," Greta complained. "It's like Marc has turned him into another person."

"Are they still friends?" Ty asked. "I mean, after Artie wrecked his car and all?"

"I'm not sure," Greta answered.

"Maybe they won't run around together anymore," Liz suggested.

"I doubt it would make any difference," Greta replied. "Artie seems to have become permanently weird." She took a bite of her carrot, then tossed it down. "Okay, who has chocolate?" she demanded.

Reenie handed her half a chocolate chip cookie.

Sean cleared his throat. "I have a major announcement."

We could use a new topic of conversation, Reenie thought. Anything that doesn't involve P.J., Artie, or Marc.

"Reenie's parents are going to be away for a few days," Sean announced. "I'm trying to talk her into throwing a Christmas party."

"Hey, awesome!" Ty exclaimed.

"Yeah, good idea!" Greta agreed.

"I'll come," Liz added.

"It's unanimous," Sean declared. "Everybody thinks you should do it."

"I'll think about it," Reenie told them. "But—I'm not sure—"

"Come on, Reenie," Greta urged. "You can't let a chance like this slip away."

"No one else's parents are going to be out of town right before Christmas," Sean added. "This is too good a chance to pass up."

They all gazed at Reenie, waiting.

Reenie had suggested the idea to Sean as a "maybe" kind of thing. But she wanted to have the party as much as everyone else did. She was up for anything that would help get things back to normal.

"Okay," she replied, grinning. "Let's go for it."

"Who are you going to invite?" Greta asked.

Before Reenie could answer, Sandi Burke pushed her way up to their table. "Get to the weight room," she choked out. "Quick!"

Reenie felt a chill down her back. Something else has happened, she knew. Something bad.

"What's wrong?" Sean asked Sandi.

"What happened?" Liz demanded.

"Just get to the weight room," Sandi replied, her eyes wide with fear.

Chapter 14

KISS OF DEATH

*R*eenie bolted down the corridor to the gym. Sean yanked open one of the big double doors, and they all raced to the weight room.

"Stay back!" Coach Wilkins ordered sharply as they crammed inside. Reenie caught his expression of alarm.

She stood on tiptoes, straining to peer around Coach Wilkins and the group of kids crowding the small room.

She cried out when she saw Artie lying beside the weight-lifting bench. He was sprawled on his back, arms and legs splayed. He didn't move.

Is this another joke? Reenie wondered. No. Coach

Wilkins wouldn't get involved in one of our stupid pranks.

"Artie!" Greta screamed. She shoved her way through the crowd, trying to reach him.

The coach grabbed her by the arm. "I told you to stay back!" he snapped. "He needs air."

Reenie turned to Sandi. "What happened?"

Sandi's words came in a rush. "We were talking in the hall, Artie and me. He started bragging about how much weight he could lift—you know, in a bench press or whatever you call it—and I didn't believe him. He said he'd show me. And Artie asked P.J. to help with the weights if anything goes wrong. You know. To be his spotter. I think he wanted to make P.J. feel bad. P.J. would never be able to lift as much weight as—"

"But what happened to Artie?" Greta demanded impatiently.

"Artie lifted the barbell off the stand okay," Sandi explained. "But then he couldn't get it back on. His arms were giving out. He yelled for help, but P.J. didn't know what to do, or he wasn't strong enough—or something. P.J. dropped the barbell on Artie. Artie fell off the bench, and the weight fell on top of him!"

Artie groaned.

He's alive! Reenie told herself. She wrapped an arm around Greta's shoulders.

"Where do you hurt?" Reenie heard Coach Wilkins ask.

"Everywhere," Artie groaned. He struggled to sit

77

up. "I'm going to get that little creep, P.J." he threatened.

"You are going to stay put. I have a doctor on the way," the coach told him. "You both should have known better than to fool around in here without supervision."

Reenie glanced around the weight room. She spotted P.J. sitting against the back wall, staring down at the floor. Liz knelt beside him, an angry expression on her face.

"I feel sorry for P.J.," Greta declared. "He was only trying to help. Artie never should have asked him. He should know P.J. can't do things like that." She hurried over to P.J. and Liz.

Whoa, Reenie thought. That's no way to calm Artie down. He's going to explode if he catches Greta over there with P.J. He's already so jealous.

"Don't try to stand up until I get back," Coach Wilkins instructed. "Do you understand me, Artie?"

Artie nodded. But the second the coach left the room, Artie struggled to his feet.

Reenie knew the exact moment he spotted P.J. His face turned the same dull red it had after the car crash.

Nothing is going to stop him from going after P.J. this time, she thought. Nothing.

"You little jerk!" Artie bellowed. "What were you trying to do—kill me?"

"Please, Artie," Greta begged. "Leave him alone."

Liz jumped to her feet and stood in front of P.J. as if to protect him.

"Leave poor little P.J. alone," Artie mimicked sarcastically. "Poor little P.J. who tried to kill me."

"It was an accident!" Greta cried. "Just an accident. He isn't strong enough to lift those weights and you know it." Then Greta added in a sweeter, calmer voice, "Come on, Artie. Accidents happen."

"Yeah, that's right," Artie said coldly. He stared menacingly at P.J. "Accidents happen."

With a loud groan Artie dived for P.J.

P.J. scrambled to his feet. He stared frantically around the room.

Greta threw herself between P.J. and Artie. "Don't touch him!"

Bad move, Greta, Reenie thought. Now he'll want to get P.J. even more.

"Defending your new little boyfriend? How sweet!" Artie tried ducking around Greta to get to P.J. But she blocked his path.

Coach Wilkins burst through the door. "Stop right there," he ordered. He strode up to Artie and held him roughly by the arm.

"P.J., get to your next class," the coach ordered. "The rest of you, too. The show is over. The doctor wants to examine Artie. Without an audience."

Liz and Greta hovered beside P.J. as they all filed out of the room.

Reenie glanced back at Artie. His eyes were focused on P.J., the muscles in his jaw clenched tight. This isn't over, she thought. This definitely isn't over.

* * *

"Sorry I'm late, guys," Artie muttered. He plopped down on Reenie's bed next to Greta and took a swig of her Diet Coke. Then he leaned forward and gave her a long kiss.

Interesting, Reenie thought. I guess they made up—for the millionth time since they started going together.

"How come you're late? You found something you would rather do than study trig?" Sean joked.

"I wanted to get in my weight training. I skipped it yesterday," Artie explained.

"Weight training?" Greta asked. She didn't sound too happy. "After what happened in school this afternoon? I didn't think you were still doing that."

"Yeah," he admitted. "But not at school. Marc's got his own set of weights—better than the ones in the gym. I work out over there now."

"I thought Marc was steaming because of what happened to his new car!" Greta exclaimed.

"He finally cooled off. He realized it was P.J.'s fault. Everything bad that's been happening to me is because of that guy. What a bad-news guy. It's not safe to be around him."

Reenie noticed that Greta didn't jump in to defend P.J. She must not want to start another fight, Reenie decided. I don't blame her.

"Well, we're all here except for Ty," Reenie announced. "He called to tell me he's going out with Liz tonight. He tried to sound casual about it. But I could tell he thought it was a big deal."

"Took him long enough," Artie commented.

"He finally did it. Cool," Greta remarked. "I told you they're perfect for each other."

Sean sighed. "Can we go on to the next problem? We can discuss Ty's love life later."

"Nope. We have something more important to do first," Reenie replied.

Artie squinted at her. "Excuse me?"

"We have to decide who to invite to my party!" Reenie explained. She picked up a pad and pencil. "Come on. Let's hear some names."

Greta laughed. "That's much more important than trig," she agreed. "How about Deena Martinson?"

"Corky Corcoran," Sean recommended.

"And Julie Prince," Greta added.

"Hey," Reenie said, "aren't you forgetting something? We've got to invite some guys, too. How about Gary Brandt?"

"Bobby Newkick," Sean called out.

"Nooooooo!" Reenie and Greta moaned in unison.

"Guess not," Sean concluded.

"Wait—I know!" Greta exclaimed. "Reenie, you've absolutely got to invite—"

Artie interrupted her. "My first choice is P.J."

They all stared at him.

Artie grinned. "You've got to invite P.J.," he insisted. "The party won't be nearly as fun without him."

"Oh, come on," Reenie answered.

"Marc and I have a little surprise for him. Your party is the best place for it." Artie grinned mischievously.

"No way!" Reenie protested. "No dumb tricks at my party!"

"What are you two planning?" Greta demanded. "I'm not going along with anything that might end up with P.J. getting hurt."

"Your little P.J. won't get hurt. I promise. We're just going to play one of our tricks on him."

I don't want this, Reenie thought. "What kind of trick?" she demanded.

"Hey, this is going to be way cool. Trust me," Artie said. "Sandi Burke is probably the hottest date in school. Do we all agree?"

"Hey—I thought I was," Greta complained.

"You are. But you're taken." Artie looped his arm around Greta and pulled her closer to him. "It turns out Sandi owes Marc big time. I don't know all the details. But Marc got her out of some mess with her parents. Anyway, Marc asked her for a favor, and she said okay."

"Get to the point," Sean urged.

Artie smirked. "Sandi is going to ask P.J. to Reenie's party."

"She's going to ask *him?"* Sean cried.

"No one would believe that," Reenie protested.

"P.J. would," Artie replied. "The guy's so weird he'd probably believe anything."

"So P.J. comes to the party with Sandi. Then what happens?" Sean asked.

"Sandi will give P.J. a long, hot kiss—a real sizzler! Right in front of everyone. Then she's going to fall on the floor and pretend to die."

"I don't get it," Reenie said.

"P.J. will think his kiss was too hot to handle!" Artie exclaimed, laughing.

"Classic!" Sean cried. "Classic! It's awesome! Especially if we all pretend she's really dead!"

"It's dumb and mean," Greta said. "It's the dumbest thing I ever heard!"

"It's like the tricks we pull on each other all the time," Sean reasoned. "It might make P.J. feel like he's fitting in."

"It's too dumb," Greta insisted. "Why spoil the party with something so stupid?"

"Maybe we should stop our practical jokes," Reenie added. She shuddered. "I almost drowned the last time, remember?"

Artie flushed. "That was stupid of me and Marc," he murmured. "But what could happen to P.J. in your living room with all of us right there?"

I guess if Marc and Artie have to get even with P.J., a joke is the best way, Reenie thought. "It would be kind of funny to watch his expression when Sandi drops dead from his kiss," she admitted.

"I can just picture it." Artie started wringing his hands and shivering. "I-I g-guess I was too m-much m-man for her." He cracked up. So did Sean.

Reenie and Greta held out for a second. Then they exploded into giggles.

"I can't wait to see what he does!" Artie exclaimed.

"The kiss of death!" Sean shouted.

Artie laughed so hard, he toppled over onto the floor and lay there, clutching his side.

"Whatever you do, don't let Liz find out," Sean cautioned when they got control of themselves. "She would tip P.J. off for sure."

"Okay," Reenie agreed. "But afterward we have to remind them that we play these jokes on each other all the time. I don't want Liz to think we're picking on P.J."

"Definitely," Greta agreed.

"I can't wait for the party!" Artie declared.

"The kiss of death!" Sean said in a deep, sinister voice.

The others repeated it after him. "The kiss of death!"

Chapter 15

THE PARTY

I know I didn't invite this many people, Reenie thought, staring around at the crush of kids in her living room.

The doorbell rang again. When Reenie answered it, Ty and Liz stepped in, stamping snow off their shoes. She couldn't remember the last time she'd seen them apart.

"Merry Christmas!" Liz exclaimed.

"Merry Christmas! Give me your coats and I'll stick them in my room." Reenie held out her hands.

Ty helped Liz off with her coat and handed it to Reenie along with his jacket.

"Great dress," Reenie told Liz. "And it almost matches Ty's shirt. You haven't started shopping at Two Cute, have you?" she teased.

"No way!" Ty laughed, embarrassed. "It was an accident. We don't dress alike. Really."

"There's pizza in the kitchen," Reenie said. "Sean is around someplace—talking chess strategy or something. Artie and Greta are here already, too. Have fun, guys."

Reenie wove through the crowd and down the hall to her room. She tossed the coats onto her bed, then headed to the kitchen for more chips.

Sean reached out and grabbed her by the waist as she hurried by. "How do you think it's going?" she asked. "Do you think everyone is having a good time?"

"Everyone but you," Sean answered. "Let's dance."

"The chip bowls are almost empty," Reenie protested. But she wrapped her arms around his neck.

"Yeah, three people have fainted from hunger already," Sean said, rolling his eyes.

There wasn't enough room to do more than sway back and forth to the music. But that's fine with me, Reenie thought. She closed her eyes and rested her cheek against Sean's sweater.

"Any sign of P.J. and Sandi?" she asked when the song ended.

"Haven't seen either one of them," Sean replied.

"Maybe Sandi changed her mind. Or P.J. wouldn't go with her," Reenie said.

She half hoped they wouldn't show up. The party

was going great. And the stupid joke could spoil everything if P.J. took it the wrong way.

"Any more chips, Reenie?" Ricky Shore called from across the room.

"Told you I had to get refills. I'll be back in a second." Reenie slipped away from Sean and headed to the kitchen.

"She's grounded until she's twenty. Her mother caught her smoking," Reenie heard someone say as she passed by.

Who were they talking about, Reenie wondered. She glanced around the room. Still no sign of Sandi or P.J.

"It was great!" Megan Carman was exclaiming to two other girls. "The game was tied with two seconds to go," she explained. "And Gary Brandt took a shot. The ball bounced on the rim, and the buzzer sounded. And the ball kept bouncing. And then it fell in. After time had expired. But it still counted!"

Reenie spotted Artie. She crossed over to him. "Are Sandi and P.J. coming?" she asked.

"Definitely," a husky voice said in her ear.

Reenie whipped her head around. Marc grinned at her. He stood so close she could smell the beer on his breath. She could see exactly where the scar on his forehead began and ended.

Reenie backed up a few steps. She didn't feel comfortable standing so close to Marc.

"How much longer before they get here?" Artie asked. His eyes looked watery.

Great, Reenie thought. They've both been drinking.

"Not long. I just called Sandi's house. Her mom said they left already."

Reenie edged away. She felt guilty that she hadn't told Liz about the joke they had planned for P.J. The more she thought about it, the more it bothered her.

Reenie passed a couple making out in the hall. Then she noticed Liz standing by herself. Before she could change her mind, Reenie hurried over.

"Great party," Liz said. "Ty's getting us some Cokes from the kitchen."

"Liz, there's something I need to tell you. P.J. will be here any minute, and—"

"He told me he wasn't coming to the party!" Liz exclaimed.

"How long ago did he tell you that?"

"A few days ago. Why?"

"Because he's coming with Sandi Burke."

"P.J.?"

"She asked him to bring her," Reenie explained.

"Sandi did?" Liz sounded amazed. "He never mentioned anything about it."

"I don't know why he didn't tell you. But he's coming with Sandi. And it's a trick—one of our dumb jokes." Reenie forced herself to meet Liz's gaze.

Liz frowned. "What kind of a trick? What are you going to do?"

Reenie told her the whole plan.

Liz's eyes widened. "Oh, no!" she cried. "Reenie, how could you do this? You know how shy he is. And I told you about his health problems."

"It . . . it's no different than the jokes we play on each other all the time."

"It's a *lot* more different than you know!" Liz cried.

"Liz, I'm sorry. It—"

"You did this behind my back!" Liz sounded furious. "How could you go along with this, Reenie? How could you be so cruel?"

"I . . ." Reenie didn't know what to say.

"Maybe I can stop P.J. before he gets here," she declared. She darted toward the door, then whirled around to face Reenie. "You have no idea what you've done, Reenie. No idea at all."

She pulled open the door and rushed out into the night.

"Reenie?"

She turned to find Ty holding a Coke in each hand. "Was that Liz?" he asked.

Reenie nodded.

"Where did she go?" Ty looked puzzled—and a little hurt.

Before Reenie could answer, the sound of the party abruptly changed. The loud babble of voices became a low murmur.

Suddenly everyone was staring at the door.

P.J. and Sandi had arrived.

"What is she doing with *him?*" Reenie heard someone whisper.

"Yeah, I thought Sandi only dated within her own species!" someone joked.

Reenie saw Ty slipping out the door behind them.

He's going after Liz. Good. I hope he can convince her that we're not trying to hurt P.J.

Sandi took off her coat and handed it to P.J. P.J. kept his on. He was wearing only a denim jacket.

He must be freezing without a heavy coat, Reenie thought. Then she turned her attention to Sandi.

Wow! In that dress Sandi should be in an MTV video—not at *my* party, Reenie thought. The short black dress showed off Sandi's long legs. She wore a sparkly red vest. She had on heels and sheer black stockings.

"Whoa!" a guy near Reenie murmured.

P.J.'s eyes darted nervously around the room. He appeared tense.

This is a big mistake, Reenie thought. P.J. is never going to understand. He's going to feel humiliated. Why did I agree to this?

"Hi, everybody!" Sandi exclaimed.

P.J. said nothing.

"Hey, P.J.," Marc called. "What's your secret? I've been asking Sandi out for months—but she always tells me to get lost."

P.J. shrugged. A sly smile spread over his face. "I don't know."

"I asked him!" Sandi declared.

"No way!" Marc yelled. "She asked you?"

Sean joined Reenie. "Marc better cool it," he whispered in her ear. "If he embarrasses P.J. too much, P.J. might leave. Then we'll never get to the good part."

90

Reenie experienced a new rush of doubts. "I'm not so sure this is a good idea," she told Sean.

"It's too late now. P.J. will be okay," Sean assured her.

He's right, Reenie decided. It's going to happen, no matter what.

"Where can I put my coat?" Sandi asked.

"I'll take it," Reenie said.

She took the coat from P.J. and dumped it on her bed with the others. She rushed back to the living room and over to Sean. She wanted to be with him, in case . . .

In case what?

What was she afraid of?

Greta popped a CD into the player. Then she grabbed Artie and they started to dance. Before long the room was full of shifting, dancing bodies.

"Want to dance?" Sean asked. "I like this song."

Reenie shook her head. "Later, okay? I'm too nervous."

She couldn't stop thinking about what Liz had said. She sounded so hurt and angry. *You have no idea what you've done, Reenie. No idea at all.*

But what have I done? Reenie asked herself.

"Check it out," Sean whispered.

Sandi Burke towed P.J. into the middle of the dancing couples. She pulled him to her and began moving with the music. P.J. had no choice but to move, too.

He was stiff. Awkward. A few kids snickered. The other dancers gave them room. Everyone watched.

He's terrified, Reenie realized.

Sandi pushed herself against him, whispered in his ear. P.J. blushed.

I never should have gone along with this, Reenie thought. Liz will never be my friend again.

Finally the song ended. "You were wonderful!" Sandi exclaimed loudly.

She pulled P.J.'s face to hers.

Kissed him.

A long, slow kiss.

P.J.'s hands fluttered at his sides.

Staring at Sandi, Reenie thought of a vampire. A vampire sucking the life out of its victim. She was kissing the helpless P.J. so intensely!

Reenie saw him try to back away. To pull free.

But Sandi held on, her mouth moving over his, her arms wrapped tightly around his slender shoulders.

"Whoooooooa!" someone cried.

Some kids laughed uncomfortably. Some whispered. Some cheered.

Suddenly Sandi stiffened.

She appeared to shove P.J. away.

Reenie saw the startled expression on P.J.'s face.

To everyone's surprise, Sandi tossed her head back and uttered a long, frightening moan. Almost an animal howl.

She sank to her knees, her eyes wide, her mouth hanging open,

Kids gasped and cried out.

Sandi crumpled into a heap on the floor.

"What happened?"

"Somebody help her!"

"Do something!"

Alarmed cries rang out through the living room.

Artie and Marc rushed to Sandi. They dropped down beside her and looked at her curiously.

"Give her air! Give her air!" Marc demanded.

Artie shook Sandi's shoulders. He shook her hard.

"Hey—!" Artie cried. "Hey! Hey!"

He shook Sandi. And waited. Shook her again.

Too hard, Reenie thought. Why is he doing that? Why is he shaking her so hard?

Artie shot Marc a terrified look.

Why does Artie look so frightened? Reenie thought. Why doesn't he end the joke? Reveal it to everyone? It's taking too long.

"Noooo." A howl escaped Marc's lips.

Artie shook Sandi by the shoulders. Then he started pumping her chest with both hands, pounding down frantically, desperately, as if giving artificial respiration.

"Artie—this is going too far!" Reenie finally choked out. "Give us a break!"

She saw P.J. backing away, his pale face twisted in horror.

"Nooooo!" Another mournful howl escaped Marc's lips.

Sandi's head bounced against the floor as Artie pounded her chest. She didn't blink. Her eyes stared blankly at the ceiling.

Kids were whispering softly. No one moved.

"Come on, Sandi! Come on! Come on! Come on!" Artie chanted.

Then with a cry he leaped to his feet. His eyes swept over the startled crowd.

"Hey! This was supposed to be a joke!" Artie cried in a shrill, trembling voice. "A joke. Just a joke. But—but—Sandi's dead! She's really dead!"

Chapter 16

ANOTHER SURPRISE

P.J. stared down at Sandi, his eyes wide with confusion and horror. "But—I—I didn't do anything to her!"

"She's dead!" Artie shouted, glaring up at P.J. "You—you *killed* her."

P.J.'s mouth moved as if he wanted to speak, but no words came out.

Poor P.J., Reenie thought. He has no idea this is all a joke. Should I tell him?

No, she decided. It's too late. They will only tease him more if I try to protect him.

Reenie spotted Greta across the room. Their eyes

95

met. Greta pressed her lips tightly together and shook her head.

"We have to call the police!" Marc insisted.

"I . . . I . . ." P.J. stammered.

"Quick! I mean it! Somebody call the police," Marc commanded.

"Must have been one hot kiss!" one of the cheerleaders joked.

"Killer kiss," Sean muttered.

Reenie could tell the other kids were trying not to laugh. They knew Sandi was okay. If P.J. glanced down, he would notice her chest rising and falling, too.

Come on, P.J., Reenie silently urged him. Don't let them make a fool out of you. Look at Sandi. She's not dead. She's about to burst into giggles.

P.J. uttered a low moan from deep in his throat. His eyes rolled up in his head until only the whites showed. His body started to convulse.

Oh, no! Is it his heart? Reenie wondered. She rushed toward him.

Greta let out a scream—high and piercing.

"Shut up!" Artie snapped.

Shaking all over, P.J. crumpled to the floor at Reenie's feet.

Sandi sat up, a confused expression on her face. "Hey! You guys went too far. You really scared him!"

Reenie leaned over P.J. and pressed her ear against his chest. All she could hear was her own pounding heart. It thudded painfully inside her.

"I'm going to bring him some water," Greta called.

It's my fault! All my fault! Reenie thought. I'm the only one who knew he had a heart murmur. I could have stopped this if I tried. How could I have been so dumb?

"You told me it would be funny!" Sandi cried. "But no one's laughing!"

"Sean!" Reenie yelled. "I think P.J. is—I think P.J. is—"

Dead. She couldn't choke out the word—but that is what she thought. She thought P.J. was dead.

Sean rushed over and crouched next to Reenie. "I can't hear a heartbeat," she whispered.

"P.J. only fainted," Artie said. "I'll show you." He knelt down beside P.J. And shook him the way he had shaken Sandi.

"Come on, P.J.," Artie pleaded. "Don't be a wimp. You can't be that scared." He shook P.J. harder. Shook him until P.J.'s head flopped back and forth on his shoulders.

Greta returned with a glass of water. She cradled P.J.'s head in one arm and tried to pour the water into his mouth.

He didn't swallow. He didn't choke. The water ran down his chin and cheeks.

"No!" Greta cried. "No, no, no."

Sean grabbed P.J.'s wrist. The crowd grew silent. "I don't feel a pulse," he reported.

"Don't die on me, man," Artie moaned. "Wake up. P.J. Come on. Snap out of it. *Please!*"

"Marc, call 911," Reenie ordered. Marc didn't move. Dazed, he stared down at P.J.

P.J. lay there. Pale. Not moving.

Not moving or breathing.

Reenie shuddered. Sean pulled her close, held her.

"He's dead," Reenie wailed. "We killed P.J."

PART THREE

1965

Chapter 17

BETH AND JEREMY

*T*he car had flipped upside down. Beth hung from her seat belt with Jeremy suspended beside her.

"Jeremy," she called in a choked whisper.

No answer.

She found the release on her seat belt and pressed it. She dropped to the floor. Actually the roof, she reminded herself.

Okay, what do I do? Beth asked herself, trying to calm down. What? Free Jeremy? Get out of the car? Get help?

She found the release on Jeremy's seat belt. Pushed. Nothing happened. She tried again. The belt let go with a snap, and Jeremy landed with a thud.

I'm not hurt, Beth realized. We had a horrible accident and I'm not hurt!

Beth stared over at Jeremy. Bright light filled the car. She realized the headlights were still on. Reflecting off the snow.

No blood! No cuts. No open wounds. Relief swept through her. He's okay, too.

Beth spotted the only way out of the crumpled car. The passenger-side window. The glass had been knocked out in the accident. She wriggled through the window and landed in the snow.

Now I have to save Jeremy.

She stretched out flat on her stomach in the snow, then reached in to grab Jeremy's arm. She tugged as hard as she could.

Jeremy moved a little.

Beth pulled with all her strength until she slid Jeremy to the window. Now for the hard part. She clutched his coat and yanked.

She pulled one arm out. Then his head. Then his shoulders. She pulled on his coat again—and the rest of his body slid out all at once.

"Jeremy!" she cried. "Wake up. Please."

He groaned and opened his eyes, blinking in the silvery light "Wh-what happened?"

"We were in an accident. You lost control of the car and we went tumbling down a steep hill. Don't you remember?"

Jeremy stared at her blankly. "Yeah," he muttered. "Yeah, now I do."

"Are you all right?"

"I . . . I'm not sure."

He sat up slowly. "Nothing hurts. I guess I'm okay."

Beth uttered a sigh of relief. "Me, too."

"We've got to get back to that boy!" Jeremy urged. "Maybe it's not too late to help him." Jeremy struggled to his feet.

"Are you sure you should stand up?"

"Yeah, I'm fine." He reached down and pulled Beth to her feet.

"Hurry," he urged. "We've got to find that boy. Right away."

They stumbled through the deep snow. Beth couldn't see the road. She hoped they were heading in the right direction.

She glanced back at the car. It was a crumpled mess. The tires in the air. The roof flattened against the ground. The windows all shattered and reduced to slits—except the one she and Jeremy had escaped through.

How did we ever survive that? Beth wondered.

"The boy should be right about here," Jeremy said. "This is where we hit him."

No sign of him. No footprints in the snow. No skidmarks on the road.

"We must be in the wrong place," Beth said quietly.

"No," Jeremy replied. "Look." He pointed at the dark spots in the snow a few yards up ahead.

Bloodstains?

"How could he have walked away?" Beth asked.

"Oh, man," Jeremy muttered. "No way he could

have walked. Could someone have picked him up—while we were unconscious?"

"Only you were unconscious," Beth pointed out. "I wasn't. I'd have heard it if a car stopped."

"But . . . where could he have gone?"

"We can follow his tracks," Beth suggested.

They searched for his footprints in the snow.

There were none.

None at all.

"What's going on here?" Beth asked in a shaky voice. "How can this be?"

Chapter 18

A CROWDED CAR

A crunching sound nearby. A low roar.

"What's that?" Jeremy whispered.

Beth heard it, too. "It's a car!" she exclaimed. "Coming from over there."

Headlights swept over the snow as the car approached. The low roar of its engine grew louder.

Beth and Jeremy moved to the side of the road, frantically waving their arms. The car's headlights grew brighter.

But . . . but it's not slowing down! Beth realized.

"Stop! Hey—stop!" she screamed. "Emergency! Stop!"

The car roared past them, whipping snow and slush into Beth's face.

What is wrong with that guy? Why didn't he stop? Beth wondered. She watched as the car's taillights shrank to two red dots, then vanished.

"Maybe he thought it was a trick," Jeremy suggested. "Maybe he thought we planned to rob him. Or maybe he was late for a New Year's party. It is New Year's, after all."

Beth clutched his arm. "Listen, another car is coming!"

"I'm going to make sure this one stops," Jeremy said. He strode to the center of the road and turned to face the oncoming vehicle.

Beth joined him. A truck this time, she decided. She could tell by the way the ground shook, and by the sound of its diesel engine.

The truck's headlights rolled over the snowy ground.

The vibrations beneath Beth's feet grew more intense.

Beth and Jeremy frantically waved their arms over their heads.

The truck sped toward them, roaring through the silent night.

"Help us!" Beth screamed. "Please!"

Beth could see the truck's grille.

And bumper.

"Jump!" she shrieked. She flung herself out of the truck's path. Jeremy landed hard beside her.

"I don't believe it!" Beth cried. "That truck nearly flattened us!"

"He didn't even slow down," Jeremy murmured, his eyes on the vanishing taillights. "What is wrong with people tonight? Don't they have any holiday spirit?"

They picked themselves up. Beth brushed some snow off Jeremy's back. I should be freezing, Beth thought. But I'm not. Must be the shock of the accident.

"Someone has to stop," Beth murmured.

Help us, she thought. Please. Someone.

A tear trickled down her cheek. Then another. And another. She wiped them away.

Three more cars sped past them without slowing down.

"What are we going to do?" Jeremy asked. "We can't stay out here. We'll freeze."

"I saw some lights over there," Beth said, pointing.

But she couldn't find them again. Where were they? Could the trees be blocking her view? She moved to the left, peering through the trees.

And there they were! Pale white lights. Up near the top of a hill. Windows. Glowing brightly.

"It's a house!" she cried. "Whoever lives there will help us. They've got to!"

They hurried toward the distant lights. When they reached a wire fence, they climbed over and found themselves in a snow-covered field. The ground beneath the snow was uneven, and they both kept slipping.

"My boot is full of snow," she complained. But her foot didn't feel cold. Did she have frostbite?

They trudged on. The lights grew brighter. They could see the house clearly. But they had to climb over two more fences before they reached it.

"Finally!" Beth sighed as they climbed onto the wooden front porch.

Lights glowed from three windows. Someone had to be home. Thank goodness, she thought. Oh, thank goodness.

Beth pressed the doorbell. She could hear the chimes ringing inside.

They waited.

No one came to the door. Beth and Jeremy exchanged worried glances.

Beth rang the bell again. She thought she saw the curtain in the front window twitch, but no one appeared.

Jeremy knocked on the door. He pounded on it again and again.

And still no one came.

"Help!" Beth hollered. "We've been in an accident! We need help!"

"Please!" Jeremy shouted. "Let us in!"

No one came to the door.

"Why won't they open the door?" Jeremy cried.

"Shhhh! I hear something. Listen."

"I hear it, too!" Jeremy exclaimed.

"It's a TV. And people talking," Beth said.

"They're in there," Jeremy insisted. "Why are they ignoring us?"

They yelled.

Hammered their fists on the door.

Nothing happened. No one came to the door. "Why are they ignoring us? Why aren't they coming to help us?" Jeremy cried.

"What are we going to do?" Beth asked. Tears burned her eyes.

"We've got to go back to the road. Maybe some car will stop."

Beth nodded. She didn't have any better ideas. But she was too upset to move.

Tears rolled down Beth's face. Her body shook as she sobbed. Why won't anyone help us? Why, why, why?

Beth fought to control her tears. Then they turned and retraced their steps through the fields and back to the highway.

Two more cars passed.

They didn't stop. Beth didn't know what else to try. She wanted to curl up in a pile of snow and rest.

"We can get back into the car," Jeremy suggested.

"It's awfully cramped in there," Beth replied.

"At least it might keep us from freezing."

Beth couldn't argue with that.

They made their way to the car. It rested on its back, crumpled and lifeless, like a squashed bug. The headlights had grown dim, the battery nearly dead.

Beth hated the thought of crawling back inside. "The only way is to lie completely flat and wriggle yourself through the window," she explained. "I'll go first."

I really don't want to do this, she thought. But she started to slide herself into the car.

Something brushed against her face.

A hand!

"Huh? Is someone in here?" she cried, unable to hide her shock.

Beth peered into the dark car.

No.

It can't be!

"Jeremy!" she cried. "There are two people in here. A boy and a girl. And . . ."

Jeremy sounded just as stunned. "Who are they? How did they get in here?"

Chapter 19

I KNOW WHO THEY ARE

Beth stared into the darkness at the boy and the girl. Their bodies were twisted. Mangled and torn. And spattered with blood. Their eyes stared straight ahead. Unblinking.

"Jeremy—they're dead!" Beth choked out.

She stared hard at their faces.

And then shut her eyes.

I know who they are! she thought.

She backed out of the car window. Jeremy leaned down so he could peer into the car.

Beth blocked his view. "No," she told him. "Don't look. Not yet."

"Why?"

"There's something I've got to tell you first."

"What?"

She pulled Jeremy to her and held him.

"Beth—what . . . ?"

A tear rolled down her cheek. But only one. She was too stunned to cry.

"Jeremy," she whispered. "The dead boy and girl in there. I recognized them."

"Who are they?" Jeremy demanded.

She didn't know how to tell him. She could hardly believe it herself.

"Beth, who are they?" Jeremy repeated eagerly.

"They're . . . *us.*"

"You're lying!" Jeremy yelled. "No! No, Beth!"

"Jeremy, it's us in there!" she cried. "We died in there!"

"That's crazy."

"Don't you see? That's why no one will stop for us—why those people wouldn't open the door for us."

"No," Jeremy repeated. "No, no, no."

"It's true. We're dead." Maybe if I say it enough times I'll believe it myself, Beth thought.

"No!" Jeremy chanted.

He pushed Beth away and threw himself on the ground. He tried to wriggle back inside the car.

"I'll get back inside myself!" he wailed. "I'll climb back into my body!"

Beth watched, horrified, as he struggled to reach his lifeless body.

"I've got to get back inside! I've got to," he called desperately.

She watched him crawl into the car. "Please!" he begged. "Please, let me back in!"

"Jeremy—stop!" Beth yelled. "It won't do any good." She grabbed his legs and dragged him out of the mangled car.

"My arms passed right through my body!" he wailed. "I can't get back inside myself. I tried. But I can't."

"Now what?" Beth wondered. "What happens now?"

Beth saw Jeremy's mouth opening and closing as he answered her. But she could barely hear his words.

Something was wrong.

Why did Jeremy suddenly sound so faint?

"Jeremy?" she called. "What's happening?"

She couldn't hear his reply. His voice faded to silence. Then Jeremy began to fade, too.

"Jeremy!" she cried. She reached out for him. Tried to grab him, to hold on to him.

But Jeremy was gone.

Only the darkness remained.

Everywhere.

Closing on her.

Claiming her.

PART FOUR

THIS YEAR

Chapter 20

A SURPRISE BEHIND
THE FURNACE

What am I going to do? Reenie wondered frantically. She was too confused and frightened to think straight. How could this have happened?

P.J. lay dead at her feet.

Reenie stared down at him, wishing with all her might that he would groan, roll over. Scream at her. Do something. Anything.

But P.J. lay still.

Pale. So very pale.

So very dead.

Silence hung heavily over the crowded room. Then a girl began to sob.

"We have to do CPR," Sean ordered. "Reenie, you do the breathing. I'll do his chest. Everybody leave. It's not going to help to have a crowd around."

"Sean's right," Greta called. "Come on. Get your coats. We'll let you know what happened."

Reenie couldn't move. She stared down at P.J. It's all my fault, she thought. I knew P.J. had a heart murmur. I'm the only one Liz told. And I didn't say anything. Not anything. I didn't even try to stop them.

"Reenie!" Sean called sharply.

She forced herself to move. "Okay," she muttered. "First I tilt back his head—chin up. Then I clear out his mouth. Now five quick puffs of air."

Reenie lowered her head and blew into P.J.'s mouth. His lips are so cold, she thought. They are already so cold.

She pulled her head up and took a breath. Then she blew another breath into P.J.'s mouth. She could hear Sean counting—setting the rhythm between her breathing and his pumps on P.J.'s chest.

"It was supposed to be a joke!" Artie cried from somewhere behind her. "A dumb joke! Nothing bad was supposed to happen."

"Come on, P.J., live! Please live!" she heard Greta urge.

Reenie focused all her attention on Sean's counting—and her breathing. I'll keep doing it, she told herself. I won't stop until he comes back to life.

"Count, count, count, count, breath," she muttered to herself. "Count, count, count, count, breath."

Reenie felt a hand on her shoulder. She heard Sean's soft voice, telling her to stop.

No, Reenie thought. I'm not stopping until P.J. sits up. I'm not stopping.

Count, count, count, breath. Count, count, count—

Strong hands pulled her to her feet. Reenie stared down at P.J.'s body.

"He's dead, Reenie," Sean murmured. "There's nothing else we can do."

"Should I call the police?" she asked. She heard her voice quaver and she swallowed hard. "They won't blame us for P.J.'s death—will they?"

Sean frowned. "I don't know what we should do."

"We've got to do something!" Reenie cried. "We've got to call his parents. We've got to call Liz. We've got to tell everyone that—"

The window behind the couch glowed brightly as a car pulled into the driveway. Greta parted the curtains and peeked out.

"Someone's here!" she exclaimed. "Reenie—it's your parents, I think!"

"Quick—hide him!" Artie shouted. "Until we figure out what to do."

Won't that make us look even more guilty? Reenie wondered.

"We've got to get our story straight before we tell anyone," Greta urged.

"Hide him! Hide him!" Artie shrieked. He grabbed P.J.'s limp arms and started to tug.

Sean and Greta rushed to help him pick up P.J.'s body.

Reenie hesitated, then grabbed one of P.J.'s thin legs.

"Hurry!" Greta urged, watching the headlights roll over the wall. "Where can we put him?"

"The basement!" Reenie cried.

She and Sean backed toward the kitchen. The body bumped over the carpet.

"Faster!" Artie cried.

Reenie's stomach lurched as they hauled P.J. through the kitchen. Don't lose it now, she told herself. You can't lose it now.

Reenie opened the basement door with one hand and flicked on the light. She glanced over her shoulder at the steep cement steps.

"Be careful," she warned the others. "These steps are really uneven." Grasping P.J.'s ankles, she reached down with her foot and groped around for the first step. She found it, put her foot down, then felt for the next. Sean stayed one step above her.

Reenie stared up at Artie. The dim light from the basement cast shadows across his face. She couldn't make out his expression.

Don't think about anything but the steps, Reenie told herself. Don't try to decide what to do until you make it down the steps.

One of P.J.'s pantlegs slid up, and she felt the flesh of his ankle under her fingers. Cold and clammy. Dead. Reenie shivered.

She forced herself to feel for the next step and continued down the stairs.

"Where should we put him?" Sean asked when they reached the bottom.

"Behind the furnace," Reenie decided.

"I have to rest for a second," Greta gasped. They lowered the body to the ground.

"Whoa. I hate the way he's staring at me," Artie moaned. He squatted down by P.J.'s body and stretched his hand out over P.J.'s unblinking eyes.

Reenie saw Artie's hand tremble. He pressed it down and slid it over P.J.'s eyelids. "Sorry," he muttered. "Sorry, P.J."

Artie jumped back up. "Come on. Let's finish and get out of here."

They hoisted the body up and struggled over to the furnace. There was room for P.J.'s head—but not his shoulders. They had to twist him on his side and force him inch by inch into the small space between the furnace and the wall.

"Good enough," Sean declared. "We've got to get back upstairs."

They tore up the rough concrete steps. Reenie slammed the basement door shut behind them, and they hurried into the living room.

Greta rushed to the window and peeked out. "It's gone!" she announced. "The car's gone."

"Huh? Who was it?" Sean asked.

Reenie sighed. "People use our driveway to turn around sometimes," she said, shaking her head. "The next block is a dead end. And the dead-end sign is right across the street."

"Whew!" Sean breathed.

Reenie choked back a sob.

"I see how Marc and Sandi didn't bother to stay," Greta said sourly.

"What do we do now?" Artie asked.

Reenie drew in a long, shaky breath. "We have no choice," she declared. "We have to call the police. Then, I guess, they'll call P.J.'s parents."

"What will they do to us?" Greta asked.

"I don't know," Reenie answered. "But it was an accident. A horrible accident. And we have to tell them the truth."

"Reenie's right," Sean said. "We panicked. We should have called them right away."

"Let's at least bring the body back up here," Artie suggested. "They are definitely going to think we're guilty if they find it hidden in the basement."

"Who's going to make the call?" Greta asked.

"I'll do it," Sean replied.

Greta handed him the cordless phone. He dialed 911. Reenie listened as he gave the emergency operator the information. "No, I don't think he needs emergency treatment," Sean finished. "He's definitely dead."

Sean dropped the phone on the coffee table. "They'll be here in five minutes."

"That's barely enough time to get P.J.'s body back up here!" Artie exclaimed.

They pounded through the kitchen to the basement stairs.

Reenie found herself thinking about Liz. What am I going to say to her? How can I face her?

Sean led the way back into the basement and over to the furnace.

"Not much time left!" Artie crouched down and reached behind the furnace. He gasped.

"No!" Greta cried.

"Huh? What's going on?" Reenie demanded. She stared into the shadows behind the furnace.

P.J.'s body was gone.

Chapter 21

WHERE IS P.J.?

Panic swept over Reenie. She felt as if she couldn't breathe. Her legs gave way.

She leaned back against the concrete cellar wall and shut her eyes. And waited. Waited for her heart to stop pounding. For her body to stop trembling.

"We've been tricked," she finally managed to choke out.

"Yeah. Tricked," Greta murmured. She put an arm around Reenie's trembling shoulders.

"P.J. pulled a good one on us," Artie agreed, shaking his head.

"I can't believe we fell for it!" Sean added.

Greta rolled her eyes. "How could we think P.J.

died? We've pulled too many of these jokes ourselves to be fooled that easily."

"But he was so limp when we carried him," Reenie reminded them. "He was so pale, so . . . so dead-looking."

"He was faking it," Sean declared. "How else can you explain it? There wasn't time for anyone to find the body and move it."

That's the only explanation, Reenie thought. Nothing else makes any sense.

But she couldn't shake the memory of his cold skin under her fingers. His cold lips under hers as she fought to bring him back to life.

"I'm so glad he's alive." Greta's voice trembled. "I-I was really terrified."

"P.J. must be laughing his head off." Artie bounded up the stairs.

Reenie laughed. She finally began to feel normal—normal and relieved. She raced up the stairs after Artie.

"Do you know how scared I was?" Reenie asked. She threw herself down on the sofa.

"I know exactly how scared you were!" Greta exclaimed, plopping down next to Reenie. "Because that's how scared *I* was."

"I thought it might be a joke," Artie said. "All along, I thought it might."

"Yeah, right. You were scared to death and you know it," Sean said.

Artie glared over at Sean—then they both cracked up. Reenie began to laugh. Soon all four of them were laughing, slapping each other high fives, rolling on the carpet.

We're all having some kind of delayed shock reaction, Reenie realized.

Then the doorbell rang.

"I bet that's P.J. He probably wants to gloat." Reenie hurried to the front door.

She swung the door open—and found herself staring at a dark-uniformed police officer.

"I'm Officer Jackson from the Shadyside Police Department. We received a report of a death here."

"Uh . . ." Reenie didn't know how to answer.

"Did you call the emergency number?" the officer asked, fixing his eyes on hers.

"Uh . . ." Reenie repeated. "Uh, no. Everything is okay here. You must have the wrong address."

"I have to come in and check around," the officer told her.

"Sure," Reenie said quickly. She moved out of his way.

Officer Jackson strode into the room. He gazed from face to face. "All right, what's going on here?" the policeman demanded.

"It . . . it was a trick," Reenie explained. "Someone played a trick."

"You mean that someone phoned in a prank call?" He narrowed his eyes. "We treat prank calls to 911 very seriously."

"We always play tricks on each other," Sean explained. "It doesn't always work, but this time it did. Someone fooled us into thinking he was dead."

Sean explained what happened, step by step. Thank goodness Sean stayed calm, Reenie thought. She felt too shaky to explain what happened with P.J. in a logical way.

"We really believed he was dead. We wouldn't have called you otherwise," Sean concluded.

"And you're the one who lives here?" The officer shifted his eyes to Reenie.

She nodded.

"I need your permission to check the house," the officer told her.

"Go ahead," she answered. Reenie wanted him to search the house. She knew P.J.'s body wasn't down in the basement. She'd seen for herself that it was gone.

But she kept wanting to go down and check one more time. Just to make sure. Because P.J. looked so dead. Now Officer Jackson would check for her.

"Stay here," the policeman ordered before he left the room. "No one leaves."

Reenie watched the man enter the kitchen. Heard him open the basement door. Heard the *thump thump* of his shoes on the concrete step.

Reenie counted each step. Okay, he's at the bottom, she decided. Now he's crossing over to the furnace. He's bending down.

Silence.

Did he find anything?

The silence stretched out. Reenie dug her fingernails into her palms.

You know there's nothing down there, she told herself. You know it.

Reenie held her breath until she heard the *thump thump* of Officer Jackson's shoes climbing back up the stairs. He wasn't hurrying. He'd be hurrying if he found a body, Reenie decided.

"No problem down there," he reported. "But I have to fill out a full report."

The policeman recorded their names, addresses, and phone numbers before he left. Reenie didn't care what he did with them. She didn't care if he called her parents when they got home. P.J. was okay. Nothing else mattered.

No one spoke until they heard the police officer's car door slam.

"Whew!" Artie breathed.

"When he glared at me I almost confessed that I *did* kill P.J.!" Greta exclaimed. "I felt as if he could peek into my head and know every bad thing I've ever done."

"I know I sounded like a total jerk describing our dumb practical jokes," Sean added.

Reenie knew she would never want to play their game again. "Let's promise no more tricks," she said. "It's never going to be fun after tonight anyway."

"No more tricks," Greta agreed.

"No more tricks," Sean and Artie repeated.

Reenie stood up and grabbed a half-empty bowl of M&M's. "I'm going to clean up," she announced. "I don't want anything around to remind me of this horrible party."

"I'll help," Greta volunteered. She grabbed a few M&M's and left for the kitchen.

"Maybe you should only have *Halloween* parties from now on!" Artie joked. He picked up some empty soda cans and wandered after Greta. "Tonight didn't help me get the Christmas spirit," he confessed sadly.

They worked in silence until they had eliminated every trace of the party.

Greta sighed when they gathered back in the living room. "I'm beat. I can't believe we have to go to school tomorrow. I could sleep for a year."

"Me, too," Artie answered. "I'll get the coats."

Greta gave Reenie a hug. "See you tomorrow."

"Bye," Artie called.

"I guess I'll go, too," Sean said. "You going to be okay here by yourself?"

Reenie nodded.

Sean pulled her close and kissed her. Reenie wished the kiss would never end. She didn't want to think about anything but the way Sean's lips felt against hers.

"Night," he whispered.

Reenie locked the door the second Sean stepped outside. She fastened the chain, too—even though her parents never did. Then she checked every door and window.

Reenie knew she should turn the lights off, but she didn't. She felt safer being able to see every corner. She didn't need any more surprises.

She dragged herself into her room, sat on the bed, and buried her face in her hands. She felt like crying.

What a terrible night. What a terrible party.

She wished her parents were home. Or that she had asked Greta to stay with her. She didn't want to be alone.

The phone rang, startling her.

She picked it up from the nightstand. "Hello?"

"Hi, it's Liz. Is my brother still there?"

"Stop it, Liz. Please," Reenie pleaded. "We figured out the joke. We know your brother is okay."

"Excuse me? What joke? Did P.J. fall for that joke with Sandi? What happened, Reenie?"

"I'm sure P.J. will tell you all about it later—if you don't already know," Reenie replied.

"He isn't still there?" Liz demanded. "Where is he, Reenie?"

"He . . . he isn't here," Reenie told her.

Liz hung up.

Reenie forced herself to get up, and changed into her favorite flannel nightgown with the little sheep on it. Then she crawled into bed, telling herself she would brush her teeth twice as long in the morning.

But she couldn't fall asleep. She kept hearing Liz's voice in her head.

Is my brother still there? Is my brother still there?

Chapter 22

NO ANSWERS

"I didn't fall asleep for hours," Reenie told Sean on the way to school the next morning. "I kept hearing Liz's voice in my head. It gave me the creeps."

"They can't give up the joke," Sean replied. "They're determined to convince us that something bad happened to P.J." He yawned. "Oh, man, I'm wrecked this morning. I kept dreaming you guys were carrying *me* down the basement stairs instead of P.J. I tried to tell you I wasn't dead—but you wouldn't listen."

Reenie patted his shoulder. "What a horrible dream."

"I bet P.J. will be waiting for us at school—ready to laugh in our faces," Sean said.

As soon as they pulled into the student parking lot, Reenie climbed out of the car and scanned the crowd for P.J. She studied every face as she and Sean entered the school.

No P.J.

They ran into Greta and Artie in the hall. Greta didn't bother to say hi. "I haven't seen P.J. yet. But he has to be here somewhere," Greta informed them.

"I don't have any classes with him. Do you?" Artie asked Reenie.

"Fifth period. History," she answered.

"P.J. will be there," Artie declared. "He's not going to cut school for a joke that isn't fooling anybody."

Artie is right, Reenie thought. P.J. isn't the type to skip class. I'll congratulate him on tricking us, and that will be the end of it.

The first bell rang. "Talk to you at lunch," Reenie called. She continued to search the crowded halls for P.J. or Liz as she hurried to her locker and on to her homeroom.

Each class before lunch felt endless. When the bell rang at twelve-thirty, Reenie rushed to the cafeteria, hoping someone had spotted P.J. She just had to know that he'd shown up at school.

But when she met up with Sean and Greta and Artie, they told her they still hadn't found him. Or Liz. Or even Ty.

Sean and Artie started talking about a concert they all wanted to go to. Reenie tried to follow the conversation, but she grew more and more anxious.

You're being silly, she told herself. P.J. climbed out from behind the furnace. Which means he wasn't dead. Which means it was all a joke. But she kept picturing his pale, pale skin. His cold, limp body.

When the bell for fifth period rang, Reenie jumped up. "I'll let you know what happened with P.J. as soon as school is over," she promised her friends. She wished at least one of them had history with her so she wouldn't have to face P.J. all alone.

Reenie reached class before anyone else—including the teacher. Every time the door opened, she checked to see if P.J. had arrived.

Lisa Blume ambled in and smiled at Reenie. "I hear you had a pretty wild party last night."

Reenie had answered questions about the party and the joke that backfired all day. She didn't want to talk about it any more. "Pretty wild," she mumbled, then stared down at her history book.

She kept sneaking glances at P.J.'s desk. But always found it empty.

The second bell rang—and no P.J.

Reenie felt her stomach knot. Where is he? Why won't P.J. let his joke end? Is he that angry at us for playing a trick on him?

I wish I could apologize to him—and Liz. I wish he'd show up so I could tell him I'm never playing another joke. Never.

Reenie tried to focus on Mr. Northwood's lecture. Then she gave up—and stared blankly at the chalkboard. She'd make it through the class, as long as Mr. Northwood didn't call on her.

The bell finally rang. Reenie couldn't wait to tell Sean that P.J. didn't show up. She grabbed her books and rushed out the door.

Liz stood down the hall with Ty. Perfect, Reenie thought. I can apologize and check up on P.J. She hurried through the crowded noisy hallway toward them.

Wait, Reenie thought, slowing her steps. Something's wrong. Liz's face appeared red and puffy.

She's crying, Reenie realized. Crying so hard her shoulders are shaking. And Ty is trying to comfort her.

Before Reenie could get to them, she saw Liz break away from Ty and dash wildly down the hall. Ty hesitated, then followed after her.

Reenie stared down the hall after her friends. What's going on today? Why was Liz crying?

Uh-oh. The English assignment! I didn't read it. And the way today is going, we'll get one of Ms. Roper's hideous pop quizzes.

Reenie checked her watch. Still a few minutes before class. Where to go to do some rush reading?

The gym. No sixth-period classes there. Perfect. She hurried down the hall, rounded the corner, and pushed through the gym's double doors.

She climbed to the fourth row of the bleachers,

opened her English textbook, and heard something go *clink* directly beneath her. Dropped her pen.

"Figures," Reenie muttered. Her mom had given her the pen, a really good one with Reenie's name engraved on it. So Reenie had to find it.

She scrambled down to the gym floor, hurried behind the bleachers, and crawled underneath them.

The wooden bleachers rose above her in a massive framework of supports and slats. One appeared identical to another. Where had she been sitting?

Reenie heard footsteps, low voices. People entering the gym.

"He's vanished . . . vanished," a girl murmured, her voice quavering. A familiar voice. Liz's voice.

Peering between the seats, Reenie discovered Liz and Ty. They stood beneath the basketball net.

Ty gently stroked Liz's hair. "Let's drive around town and try to find out if anyone has seen him," he suggested.

"Thank you," Liz replied. She hugged him.

What is this? Reenie wondered. Could P.J. really be missing?

It feels creepy spying on them, Reenie thought. But I need to find out the truth. If P.J. really is missing, I don't know what I'm going to do.

As Reenie watched, Liz gently pulled Ty's head to hers and kissed him. A long, serious kiss.

Whoa, Reenie thought. Liz was crying so hard a few minutes ago. And now she's kissing Ty as if everything is wonderful. Why?

135

The bell rang. Liz and Ty strolled out of the gym, holding hands. Reenie spotted her pen and grabbed it. She trotted to English class.

She made it into her seat about ten seconds before the late bell sounded. "That's cutting it close," Ms. Roper warned, giving Reenie a stern look.

"You all read the assignment in *Julius Caesar,*" she stated. "Now, who wants to tell us what happened?"

No one volunteered. The teacher's eyes scanned the room, searching for a victim. Not me, Reenie pleaded, sinking lower in her seat. Please, not me.

Ms. Roper's eyes fixed on someone else. "John, you tell us what's happening in the play."

"Uh . . ." John Clayton had been at Reenie's party. He probably hadn't read the assignment, either.

"You have read it, haven't you?" Ms. Roper asked.

"Uh . . . well . . ." John stammered.

The door opened. Mr. Hernandez, the principal, stuck his head in.

"Excuse me, class," Ms. Roper said. She joined Mr. Hernandez in the hall, closing the door behind her.

A moment later she reappeared. "Reenie, Mr. Hernandez would like to talk to you."

Everyone stared at Reenie.

She rose slowly, gathering her books. She'd never been called out of class by the principal.

It had to be serious. The principal didn't call people out of class if it wasn't serious.

Reenie stepped into the hall. The police officer from her party stood beside the principal. "Sergeant

Jackson has some questions for you. Please go with him," Mr. Hernandez said. He ran his hand nervously over his thinning hair.

Wild thoughts spun through Reenie's brain. Is this about the prank call? Or something else? Has something really horrible happened?

Chapter 23

TOO FAR

The officer led Reenie to the empty cafeteria. Greta, Artie, Sean, and Sandi sat at a long table at the back. A tall, skinny man wearing a gray suit stood behind them.

"Sit down," Officer Jackson ordered.

Reenie joined her friends at the table. They exchanged worried glances.

"This is Detective Frazier," the police officer stated, nodding toward the other man. "He's got some questions for you."

The detective sat down at one end of the long table. Reenie felt her face burn when his eyes met hers. "I understand you kids like to play tricks on each other," Frazier declared. "That right?"

"They're only . . . only jokes," Artie stammered. "It's all for fun."

"Which one of you is Maureen Baker?" Frazier asked.

"I am," Reenie answered. "But everyone calls me Reenie."

"You held a Christmas party at your house last night?"

"Yes."

"And you played some of these tricks on each other?"

Reenie nodded. Why are the police questioning us? she wondered frantically. What do they think we did? Are they this upset because they think we made a prank call?

"I want to hear from each of you." Detective Frazier turned to Artie. "Tell me your name and what happened last night."

Artie told him everything. The plan to play a joke on P.J. And how they thought they had pulled it off—only to have P.J. pull an even better trick on them.

"That is what happened?" the detective asked, gazing at Sean.

"Yes," Sean replied. "Exactly."

"We always try to scare each other," Greta explained. "It's a game."

"So P.J. appeared to be dead?" The detective glanced around the table.

"Yes, and he scared me to death," Sandi confessed.

What about the rest of us? Reenie thought bitterly. Sandi didn't have to haul P.J. down the stairs.

"I . . . I didn't think he was breathing," Artie said.

"Sean and I tried to do CPR," Reenie volunteered.

"So you carried him down to the basement? But when you checked about five minutes later, he had disappeared," the detective said. "Is that your story?"

Story? Why did he call it a story? Reenie wondered. Doesn't he believe us?

"That's right," Sean replied. "And we were upstairs for only about five minutes. And P.J. was gone."

Detective Frazier listened as each of them told the same story. He repeated the same questions to each of them.

"Why are you asking us all this?" Sandi demanded. "We didn't break any laws. It was a stupid joke."

"Afraid it isn't a joke," the detective replied somberly. "We found P.J.'s jacket in the Fear Street Woods, near the lake. His sister claims he didn't come home last night."

Reenie felt her heart skip a beat. "He's . . . he's really missing?" she asked shrilly.

"Yes. He's missing," Frazier replied. "Maybe somebody's joke went a little too far."

Chapter 24

A PROBLEM WITH MARC'S CAR

"We're worried about what happened to your friend," Detective Frazier told them. "I'm giving you each my card. If you remember anything you haven't told me—important or not—call."

By the time the detective finished with them, school had let out for the day. "What could have happened to P.J.?" Greta asked as they drifted over to the parking lot.

Reenie didn't know what to think. "Why would he have been in the Fear Street Woods after the party?"

"It doesn't have anything to do with us," Sandi

insisted. "We played a joke, that's all. P.J. got into trouble after he left the house."

"Sandi is right," Sean agreed. "As soon as we left the basement, he probably sneaked up the stairs and out the back door. Then—"

"Do you think maybe someone murdered him?" Artie asked. He swallowed hard.

Reenie caught the fear in his eyes. She shuddered.

"Hold on," Sean urged. "Why are we assuming the worst? All we know is that someone found P.J.'s jacket in the woods. P.J. could be fine."

"Yeah!" Artie agreed quickly. "P.J. could be fine."

"The police don't think he's fine," Greta pointed out.

"And neither does Liz," Reenie told them. "I heard her tell Ty that P.J. had vanished. Even the police said he never returned home last night. What if they never find him?"

"P.J. has been missing for almost a week. I heard the police are planning to drag Fear Lake for the body," Reenie said. She slammed her trig book shut and flopped back on her bed. "It's making me crazy. All I can think about is P.J. I'm going to flunk all my classes."

"I know," Greta replied from Reenie's desk. "I keep wishing we hadn't played that stupid trick on him. I wish I'd taken the time to hang out with him at the party. We had some good talks, you know?"

Reenie sighed again and stared down at the cover of her trig book. "What problem are you on?"

"The fourth one," Greta answered. "But I'm not *working* on it. I'm just trying to *understand* it."

"Yuck. That problem. I couldn't do it, either. We need Sean."

Reenie tossed her book on the floor. "I wonder if we'll ever find out what happened to P.J."

"Maybe not," Greta replied. "Sometimes people disappear. That's it. Nobody ever sees them again."

Reenie shivered. She hated the idea that people could vanish. *Poof!* As if they had been snatched away to another planet or something.

Reenie decided she didn't want to talk about that. "You know what you're getting for Christmas?" she asked, determined to change the subject.

Greta stood up and stretched. "Huh? Oh, Christmas. I haven't thought about it. I guess I'm not in a holiday mood."

"Why not? Besides the obvious, I mean."

"I've decided to break up with Artie."

"No way!" Reenie gasped. "You've been a couple forever."

"I'm fed up with him. He's spending all his time with Marc, and he's going to drop out of school."

"I thought he had it with Marc," Reenie protested. "I mean, after Marc ran off and left us at the party—when everybody thought P.J. was dead."

"That lasted about two days." Greta rolled her eyes. "It's as if he's addicted to Marc or something. He can't stay away from him."

"Maybe Artie's going through a weird phase." Reenie sat up and began French-braiding her hair. "Have you checked his horoscope?" she teased.

Greta didn't smile. "He wants to work at the auto plant with Marc. He wants a car like Marc's. He claims school is a waste of time and college is for spoiled rich kids," Greta told Reenie. "Does that sound like *just* a weird phase?"

Reenie shook her head. "Sorry, Greta. When are you planning to tell Artie you're breaking up with him?"

"Every day I promise myself I'll do it. Then I wimp out."

"What do you think he'll say?" Reenie asked.

"I don't know." Greta lowered her eyes to the floor. "It's going to be so hard to tell him."

She sat down on the bed next to Reenie. "I should do it now. I'll feel better once I get it over with. Come with me—please? We're not getting any work done, and I need moral support."

"How can I help? I can't tell him for you," Reenie said.

"I don't want you to tell him for me," Greta insisted. "But if you're with me, I know I won't back out of it."

"I don't know. Is it fair to Artie? How is he going to feel if you break up with him in front of me?"

"Please, Reenie. I need your help. It's driving me crazy pretending everything is great between us. I have to tell Artie the truth."

"Okay," Reenie agreed.

"Thank you." Greta squeezed her hand. "I really appreciate it."

They grabbed their coats. "Hurry," Greta urged Reenie. "I don't want to chicken out again."

They jumped into Greta's little Civic. Greta appeared more and more nervous the closer they got to Artie's house. She sped down Old Mill Road.

"Stop sign!" Reenie called. "Stop sign!" Greta screeched to a halt.

"Sorry. Didn't see it."

Reenie felt relieved when they finally arrived. I think I'll volunteer to drive on the way back, she decided. She followed Greta to Artie's house, walking carefully on the icy walkway.

Greta hesitated outside Artie's door. Then she took a deep breath and rang the doorbell.

Artie opened the door almost immediately. Grease streaked one side of his face.

"Hi. Come on in. I saw you pull up. I was out in the garage with Marc. We're working on his car."

Greta sucked in another deep breath. "I want to talk to you about something, Artie—but not in front of Marc, okay?"

He frowned. "Uh, sure. Let me tell him he's on his own for a while."

Reenie heard the back door open and close as Artie went back into the garage.

"I hope I can do this, Reenie."

"You can," Reenie assured her.

I wish I knew what to say to her, Reenie thought. I know I'd be a mess if I had to break up with Sean.

145

Greta started to say something. But stopped as a scream erupted from the garage. A high, ragged scream of terror.

Reenie and Greta dashed through the kitchen and out the back door. The scream grew louder. The most horrifying sound Reenie had ever heard.

Greta flung open the garage door. "Noooo!" she wailed.

Reenie pushed her way into the garage. Greta and Artie stared at Marc's car.

Reenie felt an icy lump of fear slide down her spine.

A body lay sprawled over the shiny red hood.

Marc's body.

Blood dripped from his mouth and nose.

And his head . . . his head . . .

Oh, his head . . .

It was twisted around on his neck . . .

Completely backward.

Chapter 25

NO JOKE

*R*eenie fell back against the garage wall. She didn't want to look. Didn't want to see the body sprawled over the hood. The blood. The twisted, backward head.

But she couldn't turn away.

And she couldn't stop herself from imagining what had happened. The muscle tearing. The neck bones cracking.

Did Marc die with the first snap of his neck? Reenie wondered.

Did he realize what was happening to him?

Reenie gazed at Marc's face. His mouth was still

twisted into a silent scream. His eyes were wide with fear.

He knew, she realized. He knew. Finally she turned away. She couldn't bear the horrifying sight any longer.

Artie slowly backed away from the car, shaking his head. "Marc—he was fine. Fine," he insisted. "He was perfectly fine when I left him!"

Greta uttered a low moan, her eyes locked on Marc's mangled body.

Reenie felt light-headed. She swayed on her feet. She had to concentrate to keep upright.

Think, she ordered herself. Think. "We've got to get out of here," Reenie blurted out. "Whoever did this to Marc could be watching us right now!"

"He was fine," Artie repeated. "Putting in spark plug wires. He was fine. One minute ago."

"We have to call the police. Let's go!" Reenie ordered. "Don't touch anything," she said as she grabbed Greta by the arm and pulled her out of the garage, pushing Artie ahead of them.

Once inside the house, they checked the locks on all doors and windows. Reenie called 911. Then she sat down on the couch with Greta and Artie.

"It would take a lot of strength," Artie said.

"Huh?" Reenie asked. She felt numb. Artie's voice seemed to be drifting to her from far away.

"To turn someone's head like that. Whoever did it was strong—*really* strong."

"You're right," Reenie agreed.

Greta didn't make a sound. She stared blankly at the carpet in front of her.

"They had to be fast, too," Artie continued. "Marc was only alone for about a minute. We didn't even hear him scream."

"Yeah," Reenie agreed.

"It's like our game," Greta muttered.

Reenie turned and stared at her. "What?"

Greta didn't answer. She rocked back and forth, her arms wrapped around herself.

"What did you say, Greta?" Reenie demanded.

"Just like the tricks we play on each other," Greta answered in a singsong voice. "Except now someone is playing for real."

But who is it? Reenie wondered.

First P.J. Now Marc.

Who's doing it?

And then a frightening question pushed into her mind: Who is next?

Chapter 26

NOT AGAIN

*R*eenie glanced in the rearview mirror. Nothing unusual. Good.

She gripped the steering wheel of her mom's minivan. Squeezing until her knuckles hurt.

I wonder if I'll ever feel safe going out alone?

It makes sense to be nervous, Reenie told herself. It's only been a week since Marc was murdered. Just concentrate on driving. In a few minutes you'll be at the Burger Basket with Sean and Ty.

Sean's car had broken down. Bad fuel pump, he informed her. So she had to give him a ride home from work. Ty, too.

Liz had promised to pick up Ty. But she backed out

at the last minute. She felt too afraid to go out at night.

No one had been arrested for Marc's murder. And the police had no new information on P.J.'s disappearance. So the killer could be anywhere.

Reenie pulled into the Burger Basket parking lot. She checked the area carefully—no one around. She climbed out of the van, locked the door, then hurried toward the entrance.

Something moved. To her left.

Reenie walked faster.

Footsteps.

Behind her.

Reenie broke into a run.

"Hey, wait up!"

Reenie spun around. Sandi trotted up to her. "What's your problem?" Sandi asked. "Didn't you see me waving to you?"

"Sorry. You scared me. What are you doing here? The place closes in about thirty seconds."

Sandi had bundled up in a big fuzzy black coat that went all the way down to her toes. Her breath came out in white puffs when she answered. "I've come to give Ty a ride home."

Huh? Reenie thought. Sandi and Ty? What's going on here? "I, uh, I thought he was going out with Liz."

"That's why I'm here," Sandi explained, smiling smugly. "I think Liz knows more than she's saying about what happened to her brother. And I think Ty probably knows what she knows."

"Shouldn't you leave the investigating to the police?"

"I just want to talk to him. What's wrong with that?"

"Nothing," Reenie replied. "I guess."

I don't get it, Reenie thought. Why is Sandi so pumped about this all of a sudden?

Reenie stared at Sandi, trying to figure out her new attitude, as they entered the Burger Basket.

"Watch out," Sean cautioned. "The floor is slippery." He swung a wet mop back and forth across the tiles.

"Is Ty here?" Sandi asked.

"In back, straightening out the storeroom. He'll be done in a second."

"I'll wait," she told him. She tossed her coat into one of the booths. She had on a long blue sweater pulled over black tights.

Sean mopped his way to the end of the counter and stopped. "Whew! Floor's done. We won't be much longer now. As soon as we finish up in back, we can get out of here."

Sean locked the door. "We're officially closed," he announced. He slipped behind the counter and then disappeared into the kitchen.

Sandi paced back and forth across the floor Sean had mopped, leaving little damp footprints. Reenie gave her a disapproving frown. Sandi didn't seem to notice.

"My hands feel all sticky," Reenie told Sandi. "I'm going to wash them."

Being careful not to mess up Sean's freshly mopped floor any more than necessary, Reenie made her way to the ladies' room.

Reenie studied her face in the mirror as she washed her hands. I wouldn't mind being as great-looking as Sandi, she thought. But Ty is a smart guy. Could Sandi really make him tell her things by flirting with him?

Reenie dried her hands with a paper towel. She pushed open the door—and hesitated. The restaurant felt deserted. Kind of eerie, even with all the grinning Santas decorating the walls.

Come on, Reenie scolded herself. Of course it feels deserted. There are only three other people in the whole place!

Reenie hurried to the front counter.

No Sandi.

"Hey!" she called. "Where is everybody?"

No reply.

Reenie listened hard. Somewhere a small motor hummed into life. Probably a refrigerator, she thought. The restaurant remained eerily silent.

"Hey, Sean!"

Reenie's voice echoed off the yellow tile walls. Her eyes darted around. Over the empty booths. The deserted kitchen area. Sandi's still-damp footprints on the floor. The lighted menu board above the counter—Big Cheeser, $2.89; medium drink, $1.75.

"Ty!" she called.

The hollow echo of her own voice replied, followed by silence.

153

A shiver slid through her body.

"Hey, Sandi!" Reenie cried. "Where are you?"

Come on, Reenie told herself, Sandi is in the back—with Ty and Sean. Where else would they be? They'll all laugh if they realize how scared I am.

Scared?

Me?

Just because someone murdered Marc and maybe P.J.? Two people who came to my party. And who played the same game I always play with my friends.

Why should I be scared?

Another shiver swept through Reenie's body. She marched into the kitchen. No problem. Nothing to worry about.

The floor was still wet, and very slippery. Stainless-steel tables and counters surrounded her. The kitchen fan's big metal hood towered above her. For a moment she felt lost.

Where is it?

Where is the door to the back?

Then she spotted it. To her left. She turned. Lost her footing on the slick floor. And fell. Landing hard on the ceramic tiles.

Reenie shook her head. Boy, wasn't that graceful? Glad no one saw me. She shoved herself to her feet—and screamed.

"Not again. Oh, please! Not again."

Chapter 27

LIKE GARBAGE

*L*et this be a joke, Reenie prayed. Let this be the sickest joke one of us has ever played.

A pair of legs stuck out of a metal garbage can.

Long legs in black tights.

She inched closer to the garbage can and peered inside.

Sandi! Shoved facedown in the hamburger buns, lettuce scraps, and stale french fries. Mayonnaise dripped down one of her black legs.

Reenie screamed again. Screamed until her throat felt raw.

Feet pounded toward her. Sean and Ty burst through the door.

"What's wrong?" Sean demanded. "We were out back. The lid on the garbage bin—"

"Sandi!" Reenie choked out. "She's . . . she's . . ." Reenie pointed at the garbage can. "It's . . . it's Sandi."

Sean and Ty rushed to the garbage can and tipped it onto its side.

Sandi slid onto the tile floor in a pile of soggy lettuce, paper napkins, cardboard hamburger boxes, and half-eaten food.

"Wow!" Ty murmured. "Wow."

Reenie turned cold all over.

Sandi's eyes stared blankly at the ceiling.

But she lay on her chest. On her chest.

Her head had been twisted around backward.

Just like Marc's.

And her face held the same terrified expression. Her blue eyes wide with horror.

Chapter 28

A SURPRISING INVITATION

"Three kids we knew were murdered," Reenie said sadly. "It's almost as if someone was out to get us. Our friends. *Us!*"

"So what did everybody get for Christmas?" Artie asked the others hanging out in Reenie's room.

"Artie," Greta moaned. "Show a little sensitivity!"

"Hey, I wanted to lighten things up a little," Artie replied. "I don't know about you guys, but I could use a laugh."

"I'm sure it has something to do with our game," Greta stated. "Three people are dead. And they were all involved in one of our practical jokes. What other connection is there between P.J., Marc, and Sandi?"

"I have an idea," Sean announced. "It came to me while I was putting the new fuel pump on my car—and remembering what happened to Marc while he worked on his."

Reenie shuddered, trying to block out the image of Marc's mangled body.

"Tell us," Greta urged.

"I think P.J. is the killer," Sean stated.

"But . . . he's dead!" Reenie exclaimed.

"Is he?" Sean asked. "Anyone seen his body?"

"He's been missing for weeks," Reenie pointed out. "The only thing the police ever found was his jacket—in the woods. He *has* to be dead."

"No, wait. I understand what Sean means!" Greta said. "P.J. is out there, hiding somewhere—and killing us one by one."

"P.J.?" Artie shook his head. "Come on. The guy is a wimp. He couldn't kill anybody."

"Think about it," Sean urged. "He had a reason to want both Sandi and Marc dead. They played the biggest part in humiliating him."

"But how did he get into the Burger Basket?" Reenie asked. "The door was locked."

They exchanged glances. They'd talked about that for hours after it happened. But none of them knew the answer.

"I don't know how he got into the Burger Basket," Sean admitted. "But someone managed to find a way. Why not P.J.?"

"He's very smart," Greta reminded them.

"P.J. is really Houdini," Artie suggested. "Back from the grave and roaming the streets of Shadyside."

Reenie glared at Artie. "Do you want to be next?" she demanded. "Do you want to end up with your head twisted around? How can you joke about this?"

"Sorry," Artie mumbled.

Reenie sighed. "I'm sorry, too. I've been going nuts thinking every person I see is the killer. I've even wondered about Ty."

"Ty?" Greta cried. "No way."

"But he was in the Burger Basket when it happened. And we hardly ever see him anymore," Reenie declared.

"No," Sean protested. "I was with Ty from the time I left you and Sandi out front until we heard you scream."

"He hasn't been hanging around with us because of Liz," Greta added. "They're together all the time now. And we know why Liz is avoiding us."

"I think P.J. is getting his revenge," Sean told them. "And maybe he's not finished. Maybe he's after all of us."

"But where is he hiding all this time?" Reenie demanded.

"Maybe Liz is hiding him," Artie suggested. "He could be right there in his own house!"

"The police must have checked the house," Reenie pointed out. "It's probably one of the first things they did."

"Well, I think it's P.J., and I think he's hiding somewhere," Sean insisted.

"Like in a cabin in the woods!" Artie exclaimed. "There are a bunch of them out by Fear Lake. They're all empty. No one uses them in the winter."

"What should we do?" Reenie asked. "Go to the police?"

"Why would they listen to us?" Artie demanded.

"Artie's right," Sean agreed. "All we could tell them is that we *think* P.J.'s the killer, and we *think* he's hiding somewhere. They wouldn't pay any attention to us."

"So, what do we do?" Reenie asked.

"Maybe we should take turns following Liz," Greta suggested. "She might lead us to P.J."

"Let's try to talk to her first," Sean said. "Liz won't tell us anything that would hurt P.J. But we might be able to find out if she believes he's dead—and if she blames us."

"Good idea." Artie jumped up and began pacing around the room. "Because if P.J. is the killer, I'm at the top of his list."

"Maybe you should talk to her alone, Reenie," Greta said. "You're the closest to her. And she's not going to say much in front of a group of people."

Reenie glanced from face to face. They all want me to do it, she realized. "Okay, I'll try. But I'm sure Liz hates me after what happened at my party."

A light snow began to fall as Reenie pulled up in front of Liz's house on Fear Street. She put the minivan in Park and sat there, reluctant to get out.

She scanned the neighborhood. Snow covered the

roofs of the houses and the lawns, making everything white except the windows. The windows seemed to stare at her like dark eyes.

Reenie shivered. I don't like Fear Street, she thought.

So go talk to Liz. Then you can leave.

Reenie climbed out of the minivan and turned up Liz's front walk. Halfway to the house, a frightening thought occurred to her.

What if P.J. really is the killer? And what if he has been living in the house? What if he's waiting in there right now—waiting for me?

The door swung open.

Reenie jerked her head up.

Liz stepped onto the porch and stood there watching her.

Uh-oh. Too late to worry about that now, Reenie thought. "Hi!" she called as she continued up the walkway.

Liz didn't answer. She continued to stare at Reenie, her expression blank, her arms crossed over her chest.

Reenie stepped up beside Liz.

"What do you want?" Liz asked coldly.

"Well, I wanted to talk to you." This is going to be hard, Reenie thought. This is going to be so hard.

"What about?"

Reenie met Liz's hard stare. "I want to apologize. We all do. We didn't mean to hurt P.J. We didn't think anything bad—"

"My brother is missing," Liz interrupted. "He could be dead."

"I know, and I'm sorry. But we were playing a joke—that's all."

"Your apology isn't going to change anything. All I can think about is P.J. I keep imagining all the horrible things that could have happened to him. I keep picturing . . ."

Liz's voice cracked. Reenie could see tears in her eyes.

Reenie reached out to wrap her arm around Liz. Liz jerked away. She turned her back on Reenie as she struggled to control her tears.

Reenie opened her bag and fumbled around for a tissue. She tapped Liz on the arm and handed it to her.

"Thanks," Liz muttered. She sniffled. Then she straightened up and turned to face Reenie.

Reenie felt tears in her own eyes. She hadn't spent much time thinking about Liz and how she must be feeling. Everything had happened so fast—P.J.'s disappearance, Marc's murder, Sandi's murder.

"I should have talked to you right away," Reenie admitted. "We were friends, right? I should have been there for you."

Liz shook her head. "No. I didn't want you around, Reenie," Liz said softly. "I still don't. Every time I see you, I think about P.J. About what you did to my brother."

"Can't you give us all another chance?" Reenie pleaded. "Especially now, with this killer on the loose. We all need to stick together."

Anger flashed in Liz's eyes. "Go away, Reenie. I know you're sorry. But I can't forgive you for what you did to P.J. Not ever."

"Liz, I—"

Liz pulled open the storm door and dived inside. The front door slammed in Reenie's face.

"Do you think *I* should talk to Liz?" Greta asked. "Now that she's had a few days to calm down."

Reenie hesitated.

"She knows I got along with P.J.," Greta continued. They turned the corner onto Reenie's block.

"You're right," Reenie agreed. "I remember Liz wishing P.J. would ask you out. But I don't think she wants anything to do with us."

Greta and Reenie hurried up Reenie's driveway. "My feet are freezing," Reenie said. "All that slush soaked into my shoes. I want to put on some dry socks right away."

Reenie unlocked the door. They tossed their coats into the hall. "Mom, I'm home," Reenie called. "Greta's with me."

"You got some mail," her mother answered from the living room. "I put it on your bed. And I made some Christmas cookies if you want some."

"Okay. Thanks." Reenie led the way to her room.

"You want a pair of dry socks?" she asked Greta as she pulled open the top drawer of her dresser.

"No. My boots kept my socks dry." Greta plopped down on Reenie's bed.

Reenie sat next to Greta and slid off her shoes. "I wonder what this is." She picked up a long gray envelope. "No return address."

"Open it," Greta urged. "It doesn't look like junk mail. Too fancy."

Reenie tore open the envelope and pulled the letter out. She unfolded it and shook her head. "Whoa."

"What?" Greta demanded.

"I don't believe this. It's from Liz. She's inviting me to a party."

Reenie read the letter again:

December 29th

Dear Reenie,

I've been thinking about what you said, and we do all need to stick together. I need my friends to get through this horrible time.

So I've decided to have a New Year's Eve party. I know P.J. is gone, and that this has been a hard year for all of us. But let's put this year behind us and celebrate. And hope that next year is a better year for everyone.

Please come. I'm inviting all my closest friends to my house around nine.

Hope to see you then.

Liz

Chapter 29

PARTY TIME

*R*eenie peered through the car window as Sean pulled to a stop in front of Liz's house. An icy wind sent white waves of snow swirling across Fear Street.

"I don't see any lights on," Reenie commented. "And there aren't many cars parked on the street."

"You're right," Sean answered. "I wonder how many people Liz invited."

"Even if she invited a lot, I don't think many kids would come." Reenie sighed. "Justin Stiles is having a huge party tonight, remember? And his parties are always great."

"Maybe we can cut out early and head over there," Sean suggested. "Ready to go in?"

Reenie pulled open her bag and dug around for her favorite berry-pink lipstick. She waved it in front of Sean's face. "I think you kissed it all off," she told him.

"I hope you don't expect me to apologize," Sean teased.

Reenie shook her head and finished reapplying her lipstick.

"Ready?" Sean asked.

"Not really," Reenie admitted. "I'm glad Liz invited us. But I'm nervous about seeing her again."

"Come on—it's New Year's Eve!" Sean exclaimed. "Let's party!"

A horn beeped behind them. "Greta and Artie," Sean observed.

"Great! Now we can all go in together. It will be easier to face Liz in a group."

Reenie and Sean climbed out of the car and met the other couple on the sidewalk. I'm glad they didn't break up, Reenie thought. Enough bad things have happened this year.

"Party time!" Artie exclaimed. He slapped Sean a high five. "Happy New Year's Eve, guys!"

They made their way up the snowy front walk. "Haven't they ever heard of shovels?" Greta complained. "I'm going to kill myself trying to walk through snow in these shoes."

Reenie grabbed the rail as she climbed up the porch steps. She didn't want to go flying on the icy cement.

The porch light was off. Reenie didn't hear any music or voices coming from the house.

"Why is it so quiet?" Greta whispered.

Reenie shrugged and rang the doorbell. "I guess we're the first to arrive."

"Have you ever been inside?" Artie asked as they waited for Liz.

"No. I dropped Liz off a couple of times, but never went inside. And we talked on the porch the day I tried to apologize," Reenie answered. "I wonder if her parents will be home tonight. I've never met them."

Reenie hoped they wouldn't. She didn't know how she could face them. What could she say to them about the night P.J. disappeared?

"What's taking Liz so long?" Artie demanded. "It's freezing out here." He raised his fist to knock—and the door swung open.

Liz appeared, wearing a red velvet party dress. That deep red is a great color for her, Reenie thought. But Liz is so pale. Even her lips appeared almost colorless.

Liz swept out her arm, gesturing them inside. "Come in. I've been waiting for you," she said softly.

"I'm so glad you decided to have a New Year's Eve party!" Reenie exclaimed. She gave Liz a quick hug. But Liz kept her arms at her sides, her body stiff.

Why did she invite me if she's going to act so cold? Reenie wondered.

Liz turned her back on them abruptly. She walked briskly down the hall toward the only room with a light on. "The living room is this way," she called.

Oh, no! Reenie thought as she stepped into the room. She heard Greta give a little gasp behind her. I shouldn't have come here, Reenie told herself. I never should have come here.

Liz had decorated the entire room in black. Black crepe paper draped the walls. Black balloons floated at the ceiling.

It's not a party. It's a funeral, Reenie thought glumly.

"Are your parents home?" Artie asked, gazing around the room tensely.

"No," Liz replied. She didn't volunteer any other information.

Reenie glanced over at Greta. Greta rolled her eyes as if to say, "Do you *believe* this?"

Reenie studied the room, trying to appear interested in the house. But her eyes kept returning to the black decorations.

"Wow. Your living room is as big as a hotel lobby," Reenie gushed. She couldn't stand the silence one more second. Every muscle in her body had tensed.

Liz didn't reply. She stared blankly at Reenie. What is wrong with her? Reenie wondered.

The huge room was practically bare. In a corner Reenie spotted a round table with a punch bowl. Beside the punch bowl stood a large book.

"Is your family redecorating?" Reenie asked.

"No," Liz answered.

Maybe Liz's parents couldn't afford to furnish the whole place at once, Reenie thought.

"Let me take your coats," Liz said suddenly.

They handed her their coats, and she disappeared into the hallway.

"Whoa. Did we crash the Addams Family's New Year's party?" Artie burst out as soon as Liz closed the door behind her.

"Really," Sean agreed.

They stared at each other, wondering what to do. No music. No place to sit. No way to avoid the solemn, black decorations.

"How about some punch?" Greta suggested. She wandered over to the table and peered into the bowl. "At least it isn't black," she announced.

They gathered around the table as Greta filled four cups.

"So what is going on here, guys?" Reenie asked in a whisper.

"Who knows," Sean replied. "But I say we stay for half an hour and get out."

"Definitely," Artie said. "Liz is giving me the creeps. I'm not even going to try to figure out these black decorations."

"Check it out," Reenie said, picking up the big book from the table. "Liz has an old Shadyside High yearbook. What year is it? Wow—1965. I wonder if her parents went there." She flipped open the cover.

Greta snickered. "Listen to this inscription: We'll be friends until the ocean needs diapers to keep its bottom dry."

"Not too corny," Sean joked, rolling his eyes.

Reenie turned the page. "Are those the cheerleaders?" Artie cried. "Their uniforms come down past their knees!"

"Leave that alone!" Liz yelled from the doorway.

Reenie jumped. She hadn't heard Liz return. She quickly closed the yearbook.

"Why were you snooping?" Liz demanded sharply as she crossed the room toward them.

"Liz, the yearbook was on the table. I didn't think it would be any big deal. Sorry," Reenie replied.

A knock on the front door caught them all by surprise.

Great! Reenie thought. More people. More people means we can leave early. Maybe the room won't feel so creepy if it's crowded.

"Good!" Liz declared. "I didn't want to start until we were all here."

Start what? Reenie wondered. She watched Artie take a cautious sip of the punch.

"How is it?" Sean asked.

"Regular fruit punch." Artie grinned. He drank down the rest of the cup.

"Brrr!" Greta cried, rubbing her sleeves. "It's cold in here."

"I know," Reenie answered. "I don't think she has any heat on. I wish I'd kept my coat."

"Here's my date," Liz announced. She led Ty over to the others.

She sounds a little happier at least, Reenie observed. Maybe Ty will get her in a better mood.

"Yo—Ty. Where've you been, man?" Artie asked. "Haven't seen you for a while."

"Me, either," Sean said. "We keep getting different shifts at the Burger Basket."

Ty shrugged. "I haven't been doing too much. Just hanging out."

Hanging out with Liz, Reenie thought.

The room grew quiet again.

I have to ask her about P.J., Reenie decided. We can't all pretend we've forgotten what happened to him. "Any news about your brother?"

"No," Liz replied blankly, her face expressionless. "The police still haven't found any sign of him—except for his jacket."

"I hope they find him soon. We all hope he's okay," Reenie said.

Liz stared at her. A harsh, cold stare.

Believe me, Reenie silently pleaded. You have to believe that. I didn't mean for anything bad to happen. Not to P.J. Not to you. Not to anyone.

Liz turned away. "We'll learn what happened to him sooner or later—won't we," she murmured.

What is that supposed to mean? Reenie wondered. When they find his body? Or what?

"You think P.J. could have run away?" Greta asked. "Gone to another city or something?"

"No," Liz replied flatly.

"Why don't you think so?" Greta asked. "Kids our age run away a lot. I mean, it's pretty common. And he was having a tough time at school."

"I know my brother," Liz said crisply. "P.J. wouldn't want me to worry. He'd never run away."

Liz poured Ty a cup of punch and took one for herself. "It's time," she announced, waving them into the center of the room.

Time for what? Reenie wondered. It's not midnight yet.

Liz raised her cup. "A toast to our departed friends. We miss them all very much." She gazed at each person in the circle, then brought the cup to her lips.

Reenie took a sip of punch. Horrifying images of the past two months flashed through her mind. The blood dripping down Marc's cheek. Sandi sprawled on a pile of garbage. Both of their heads twisted completely backward.

And P.J. so cold and pale as she frantically gave him mouth-to-mouth resuscitation.

Would they find P.J. next? Would his head be turned around like the others?

Or was P.J. hiding somewhere? Responsible for the murders—and planning to kill again?

Liz raised her cup. "Another toast to our departed . . ." Her words trailed off. Her lips trembled and tears began rolling down her cheeks.

Liz buried her face in her hands and sobbed.

Poor Liz, Reenie thought. She's so pale. So thin. I have to remember how much she's gone through. No wonder she's feeling so emotional tonight.

Ty led Liz to a corner at the far end of the room. They could still hear her wrenching sobs.

"Do you think we should leave?" Greta whispered.

"I don't know," Reenie answered. "It might make Liz feel worse."

Reenie glanced over at Liz and Ty. They huddled close together, their backs to the others.

172

"Now what?" Sean muttered. "Should we keep pretending this is a normal party?"

"No!" Liz said loudly. "I won't."

Reenie turned and saw Liz shove Ty away from her. She strode toward them, her face twisted with anger. Her eyes almost glowing.

"I'll tell you why I invited you all here!" Liz declared.

Ty reached for her.

"Keep away from me!" she screeched.

He backed up, a hurt expression on his face.

Liz narrowed her eyes at Reenie. "The reason I gave this party is because I decided it would be easier to kill you all at once—instead of continuing one by one."

Chapter 30

REENIE DIES FIRST

"Don't try to run," Liz warned. "The doors are bolted."

"Liz, this isn't funny!" Reenie protested.

"I'm leaving," Artie declared. "I'm not playing this dumb game anymore."

Sean stared hard, studying Liz. "I don't think it's a game."

"Listen to Sean. He's the smart one," Liz told them.

"Do you mean that you killed Marc and Sandi?" Greta demanded.

"Now you're catching on," Liz replied with a cold smile.

Reenie felt goosebumps roll up and down her arms.

"No!" she gasped. "I don't believe it. You couldn't kill anyone—no matter how angry you are."

"I killed them. And I enjoyed it," Liz insisted, her eyes burning into Reenie's. "I loved hearing the *crack!* as I broke their necks. I loved staring into their terrified faces."

Artie dashed over to the big oak door leading to the hallway and yanked on it. It didn't open. He pounded on it, threw his weight against it. It didn't budge.

Greta raced to the windows at the back of the room. She shoved the curtains apart—and found wrought-iron bars.

We're trapped, Reenie thought.

"There are five of us and one of you," Artie challenged Liz. "You can't force us to stay."

"Watch me." Liz lifted the tablecloth and slid open a drawer. She pulled out a carving knife.

"Why?" Reenie pleaded. "Why are you doing this?"

"Why?" Liz fixed her gaze on Reenie. Her eyes blazed with hatred. "Because a stupid practical joke was responsible for my brother's death," she replied.

"That's not true!" Sean yelled. "P.J. didn't die at the party. He—"

"Who would like to go first?" Liz shrieked. She glanced from face to face. "Don't all volunteer at once. And don't worry—I'll get around to each of you before the New Year chimes."

Liz stepped toward Reenie. She raised the knife high above her head. The sharp silver blade gleamed. "How about you, Reenie? You want to be the first to die? You were the first to pretend to be my friend."

Liz plunged the knife right at Reenie's heart.

Chapter 31

THE SURPRISE GUEST

*R*eenie didn't have time to scream.

As the knife came down, Sean dove at Liz. He grabbed her arm and twisted the knife away from Reenie before it could stab her.

The knife clattered to the table.

Reenie stood paralyzed. She could almost feel the cold knife blade ripping into her body.

Liz shot out her free hand. Made a frantic grab for the knife.

But Sean was quicker. He snatched up the knife and pointed it at Liz.

"Get her, Sean!" Artie yelled.

"Unlock the door," Sean ordered Liz. He kept the knife aimed at Liz.

She didn't move.

"Unlock it now!" Sean barked. "I don't want to hurt you. But we're leaving—and we're getting the police."

Reenie moved closer to Sean, her heart still thudding, still feeling dazed from her narrow escape.

"Okay," Liz gasped. "Okay, I'll unlock it." She backed away from Sean. He didn't lower the knife.

Liz is giving up, Reenie thought. She closed her eyes and pulled in a deep breath, allowing the relief to sink in.

But instead of turning to the door, Liz let out a cry of attack—and threw herself at Sean.

Sean toppled to the floor with Liz on top of him.

The knife started to fall from his hand, but he grabbed it back. His body twisted and thrashed as he tried to throw Liz off.

Liz uttered another cry—and reached for Sean's throat. His face went red as she tried to choke him. "Drop the knife! Drop it! Drop it!" she shrieked.

Reenie forced herself to move. She grabbed Liz by the shoulders and struggled to pull her off Sean.

With startling strength, Liz leaned out of Reenie's grasp. Sprang onto Sean's arm—and tore at his wrist with her teeth.

Sean let out a howl of pain.

Liz cried in triumph as she pulled the knife from his grasp.

She jumped to her feet.

Sean rolled away from her, holding his wounded arm.

Liz scrambled after him. "I guess you want to be first, Sean!" she rasped, breathing hard. She slashed the air with the blade.

"Liz—don't!"

Liz froze. The knife shimmered for a second in midair. Then she grabbed Sean and pressed the blade against his throat.

"Don't, Liz!" the voice repeated.

Reenie spun around to see who was warning Liz.

"P.J.!" she shrieked.

He stepped quickly into the room.

"Don't do it, Liz," P.J. repeated.

"You're alive!" Reenie cried. "P.J.—you're okay!"

"Thank goodness you're alive!" Greta chimed in happily.

"P.J.—tell your sister!" Reenie pleaded. "Tell your sister we didn't hurt you. Tell her!"

P.J. hesitated, his eyes on Liz.

Liz kept the knife blade pressed against Sean's throat. Reenie saw a drop of red blood roll down Sean's neck.

"Liz—" P.J. moved slowly toward his sister.

Liz pulled the knife away from Sean's neck. She lowered it to her side.

"That's better," P.J. said softly, soothingly. "I'm glad you stopped, Liz. I'm glad you listened to me."

Whew! It's over! Reenie told herself. Thank

goodness P.J. arrived when he did. It's over. It's over.

A grin slowly crossed P.J.'s face as he stepped up to his sister. "I'm glad you waited, Liz," he said softly. "I would be so disappointed if you started without me. I want to watch them die, too."

Chapter 32

STABBED

P.J. spun away from Liz and faced Reenie and her friends. His eyes gleamed with hatred. "I want to watch you die. All of you!" he cried.

"But, P.J.—we're your friends," Greta insisted. "We've all been so worried about you. Where were you? What happened that night after Reenie's party?"

Behind P.J. and Liz, Reenie saw Sean slowly climb to his feet.

What is he planning to do? Reenie wondered. Be careful, Sean, she pleaded. Please—be careful.

"I've been here all along," P.J. revealed. "I wouldn't miss the fun. I watched Liz kill Sandi and Marc. She killed them—but I got to watch."

"That's sick!" Reenie cried. She hadn't meant to say anything. But the words burst out of her.

"Why?" Greta wailed. "Why did you kill them, Liz?"

Artie stepped up close to Greta.

Meanwhile, Sean crept up behind Liz and P.J.

Reenie felt sick. How could Liz be a murderer? How could P.J. enjoy watching her kill?

They seemed so normal. So totally normal.

"How could you kill Sandi and Marc because they played a harmless trick on P.J.?" Reenie asked them.

Before either of them could answer, Sean grabbed Liz around the waist. He pinned her against him with one arm—and grabbed the knife away with his other hand.

Liz spun free.

She dived at Sean.

He tried to dodge out of her way.

Too late.

Liz lost her balance. Stumbled into him.

And the knife plunged deep into her chest.

Screams rang out in the huge room.

Everyone screamed but Liz.

Reenie stared in amazement at the blank expression on Liz's face.

"Ohhhh." A frightened moan escaped Sean's throat.

Reenie knew that he hadn't meant to stab her. And now he was trembling all over, his eyes wide with horror.

Only Liz remained calm.

"N-no blood—!" Artie stammered, pointing.

Reenie gaped at the front of Liz's dress. No blood. No blood poured from the wound.

With a loud gasp Sean pulled the knife from Liz's chest.

Liz didn't move. Didn't cry out.

Reenie's body convulsed in a tremor of fear.

What's going on? she wondered. What is happening here?

Chapter 33

IN MEMORIAM

Reenie stared at the knife in Sean's hand. The blade gleamed under the ceiling light. No blood.

No blood. The words repeated in Reenie's ears until they became a roar.

Liz turned to Sean, a strange smile on her face. "You tore my dress," she told him with a phony pout.

"I-I—" Sean let the knife fall to the floor. His face tightened with fear as he backed away from Liz.

Liz laughed. "Scaredy-cat," she whispered. "So sorry, Sean. But you can't kill me. Know why?"

"Why—?" Sean managed to choke out.

"Because I'm already dead."

"Noooo!" A cry of protest escaped Reenie's throat.

"P.J. and I are already dead," Liz revealed. "We both died before you were born. Here. I'll prove it to you."

Liz strode over to the table and grabbed the old Shadyside High yearbook. She tossed it to Reenie.

Reenie's fingers shook as she ran them over the embossed cover. *Class of 1965.* She opened the book.

The glossy pages automatically fell open to a full-page photo in the front. The photo was surrounded by a heavy black border.

Beneath the photo the caption read:

IN MEMORIAM

Elizabeth Fleischer and her brother Philip Jeremy Fleischer. You will always live in our hearts.

Greta peered over Reenie's shoulder at the photograph. As she read the caption, her hand squeezed Reenie's arm.

"It's Liz and P.J.," Sean murmured, staring at the page. "Look at them! They look exactly the same. But this photo was taken over thirty years ago!"

"We weren't known as Liz and P.J. then," Liz explained. "We were Beth and Jeremy. We died in a car accident on New Year's Eve, a snowy night a lot like this one."

"And do you know why we died?" P.J. chimed in, stepping up beside his sister. "Do you know why?"

"We died because some cruel kids played a mean joke on my brother," Liz told them bitterly. "And now it's thirty years later. Thirty years that we could have enjoyed, that we could have been alive in. Thirty years later—and you kids did the same thing."

"Whoa. Wait—" Sean started.

"This time it's going to be different," Liz snapped, ignoring him. "This time you're going to pay for your joke. You're going to pay for the thirty years we lost because of a joke."

"You're all going to die!" P.J. declared gleefully.

Chapter 34

A SURPRISE FOR LIZ

"*P*.J. and I waited a long time for this moment," Liz continued. "We spent years and years trapped in a cold, gray place. As the years passed, we grew stronger. And then suddenly we were back. Back in Shadyside. Back in our old bodies. People could see us and hear us again. I realized P.J. and I had been given a second chance—a chance for revenge."

"But why take your revenge on us?" Reenie cried. "You died more than ten years before we were born! Her voice came out shaky and weak, but she forced herself to continue. "We didn't cause your death! We didn't cause P.J.'s death!"

Liz moved up in front of Reenie. She stood so close

Reenie could feel Liz's cold, sour breath against her face.

"I liked you all so much at first. Especially you, Reenie," Liz said, almost tenderly. "You were all so nice. So friendly to me." Her expression darkened. "Then you played the same kind of cruel trick on P.J. that my other so-called friends did."

She sighed. "And that's when I knew. That's when I knew you all had to die."

"We play those tricks all the time!" Greta cried. "For fun. To have a good laugh. That's all. We aren't like those other kids. We didn't want to hurt P.J." She turned to P.J. "I was your friend—remember?"

P.J. scowled. "Some friend."

"Enough talk," Liz said sharply. "My brother and I have waited so long for this. It's hard to believe it's finally going to happen."

She picked up the knife.

Smiled at Reenie. A cold smile. Dead eyes glowing.

Lurched at Reenie.

Ty jumped between them.

"Stay out of this, Ty," Liz ordered. She raised the knife, her face twisted in anger. "Move away, Ty."

Ty didn't budge. He stood there, hands at his sides, his gaze fixed on Liz.

"You've got the story wrong, Beth," Ty declared softly.

"Wrong? What are you talking about?" Liz demanded.

"You haven't figured it out, Beth," he told her.

"You haven't figured out why you were brought back to life."

"Ty, step aside," Liz ordered. "Stop trying to protect Reenie. She's going to die and so are you."

"No, I'm not," Ty insisted.

Reenie stared hard at him, studying him. She didn't know Ty very well. But here he was being so brave, so totally brave, standing up to Liz or Beth or whatever her name was. Standing up to a girl who had been dead for thirty years with such calmness, such courage.

"You haven't figured it out, Beth," Ty repeated softly. "You weren't brought back from the dead to have your revenge. I was!"

Chapter 35

HAPPY NEW YEAR

"**Y**our revenge!" Liz shrieked. "For *what?*"

"I died on that snowy New Year's Eve in 1965, too," Ty told her.

Reenie gasped.

Ty? Ty is a ghost, too? Reenie felt chill after chill roll down her body.

"Don't you remember me?" Ty asked Liz. "I remember you so well. You and your brother."

"No!" P.J. and Liz both cried at once. They are scared, Reenie saw. They remember Ty somehow.

"I didn't know why I'd been brought back to life, back to Shadyside, either," Ty continued. "Until I met you and your brother. Then I knew. I knew you were Beth and Jeremy. The ones who ran me down in the snow on New Year's Eve and left me to die."

P.J. uttered a moan of pain. "We should have stopped. We should have stopped."

"Don't!" Liz snapped at her brother. "We didn't kill him! We hit an animal. A raccoon."

"You know that isn't true, Beth," Ty insisted. "I'm sure you remember my face against the windshield. I stared in at you. I saw you both—before you raced away and left me to die."

Liz spun around and ran wildly to the door.

Ty reached it before she did and blocked her way. He stroked Liz's cheek with one finger. She shivered.

"That's why I stayed so close to you," Ty told her. "I've been waiting for this moment. The perfect moment for my revenge—New Year's."

Bong!

The clock chimed, startling Reenie. The first stroke of midnight.

"It's my turn," Ty continued. "That's why you two were brought back. So I could kill you. That's why all three of us were brought back."

An expression of pure dread spread across Liz's face.

Ty grabbed her.

Liz uttered a howl of terror.

The clock continued to chime.

Bong!

Bong!

Bong! Bong! Bong!

191

Liz flailed at Ty with her fists. Tried to wriggle out of his grasp.

But Ty held on, refusing to release her.

"Let go of my sister!" P.J. wailed.

He threw himself on Ty. Struggled to pull Liz from Ty's grasp.

Bong!

Bong!

Bong!

Reenie had lost count. But she knew midnight was only moments away.

Liz and Ty and P.J. whirled around, tugging each other as if in a mad dance.

Faster and faster.

Waves of icy air swept off their bodies. Reenie's skin felt numb. Her eyes teared.

Bong!

Liz's screams drowned out the clock.

They whirled around the vicious circle, a circle of rage and revenge.

Faster. Still faster. A ghostly whirlwind.

A high, shrill whistle pierced Reenie's ears.

Louder. Shriller. Until Reenie covered both ears to shut it out.

Then it stopped.

And the three ghosts began to fade.

They grew dimmer.

Dimmer.

Bong!

They faded to shadows.

Then the shadows faded to smoke.

A spinning column of smoke.

Bong! The clock struck twelve.

And fell silent.

The smoke faded. And floated away.

Reenie and her friends stared in shocked silence.

"They're gone," Greta whispered finally. "Gone."

Sean let out a long sigh.

Without realizing it, they were hugging each other.

Hugging each other tightly. Because they had survived.

Because they were alive!

They hugged each other in silence.

And then Reenie turned to the spot where the ghosts had spun and whirled, had done their final dance.

"It's all so sad, so sad and frightening," she said. "What more is there to say?"

For a long moment no one answered.

Then Sean put his arm around her and pulled her close. "How about Happy New Year?" he said softly.

About the Author

"Where do you get your ideas?"

That's the question that R. L. Stine is asked most often. "I don't know where my ideas come from," he says. "But I do know that I have a lot more scary stories in my mind that I can't wait to write."

So far, he has written nearly three dozen mysteries and thrillers for young people, all of them bestsellers.

Bob grew up in Columbus, Ohio. Today he lives in an apartment near Central Park in New York City with his wife, Jane, and fourteen-year-old son, Matt.

THE NIGHTMARES
NEVER END . . .
WHEN YOU VISIT

Next . . .
FEAR STREET:
WHAT HOLLY HEARD
(Coming in mid-December 1995)

Do you like secrets? Holly does. She's Shadyside High's biggest gossip—and she's always got the juiciest news.

This time she's heard a really terrible secret. She told her friends all about it. But someone didn't want Holly to know. Now someone wants to make sure Holly never talks about it again. Someone who will go to any length to keep her quiet.

Lying . . .

Threatening . . .

Even murder.

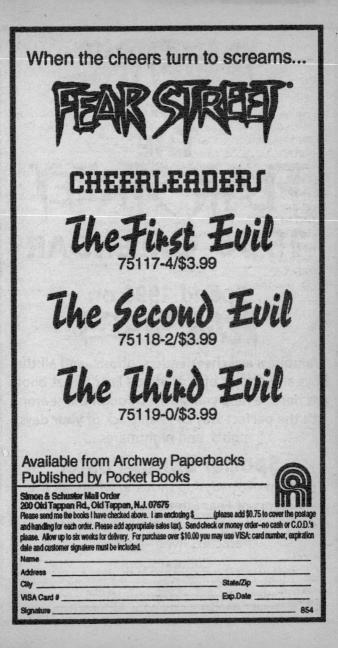

R·L·STINE

presents

THE
FEAR STREET®
1996 CALENDAR

Spend 1996 on
FEAR STREET

Vampires, evil cheerleaders, ghosts, and all the
boys and ghouls of R. L. Stine's Fear Street books
are here to help you shriek through the seasons.
It's the perfect way to keep track of your days,
nights, and nightmares....

Special Bonus Poster

A map of Shadyside showing where all the
horrors of Fear Street happened. Take a
terrifying tour of the spots where your favorite
characters lived—and died.

Coming soon

1098

A Fear Street Calendar/Published by Archway Paperbacks